WATCHTOWER RECKONING

SASQUATCH AWAKENING

LUKA T. JACOBS

Cover Design, Book Design & Formatting:
Luka T. Jacobs.

Editing: N. Harrison

ISBN: 978-1-7637810-0-9

DEDICATION

To my partner Adam and my little guy, Finnigan. Thank you for offering ideas, suggestions and for being great listeners.

CONTENTS

DEDICATION — 3

PRELUDE THE DELICATE BALANCE — 9

1 HOMECOMING — 13

2 NEVER TRUST THE HAIRLESS ONES — 17

3 A DAY'S ADVENTURE — 21

4 COVENTRY CREEK — 23

5 THE CHASE — 29

6 A HARROWING TURN — 31

7 GOOD COMPANY — 35

8 TREPIDATION — 37

9 MONSTER — 39

10 ECHO'S THROUGH THE FOREST — 43

11 CONSEQUENCES — 47

12 SHADOWS OF THE FOREST — 51

13 JUSTICE OR VENGEANCE — 55

14 BRUTAL BATTERING — 61

15 SIMPLE PLEASURES — 65

16 DEFIANCE — 71

17 DECEPTIVE PEACE — 75

18 RECKONING — 77

19	CALL EVERYBODY	81
20	LAY OFF THE HAPPY JUICE	85
21	MOMENT OF RECKONING	87
22	BUCK OUT OF LUCK	89
23	HARROWING SYMPHONY	93
24	LEAVING THE WATCHTOWER	97
25	FUTILE RESISTANCE	99
26	PATH OF DESTRUCTION	103
27	SEEK SHELTER	107
28	IT'S THE END	109
29	HAUNTING SYMPHONY OF SUFFERING	113
30	HUNTED AGAINST THE HUNTER	117
31	A DANCE WITH DEATH	119
32	UNIMAGINABLE HORROR	123
33	DON'T MAKE A SOUND	127
34	AS CRAZY AS IT SOUNDS	131
35	THE PLAN	133
36	TWISTED LOGIC	139
37	VIGILANT	143
38	RUTHLESS EFFICIENCY	145
39	EXTERMINATE	149
40	HAUNTING ECHOES	151
41	UNLEASH FURY	153

42	BEYOND THE REALM OF NIGHTMARES	155
43	FIGHT TILL THE BITTER END	159
44	VICTORY OR DEATH	163
45	FINAL STAND	165
46	SCARS OF THE NIGHT	171
47	AFTERMATH	173
48	FAMILY PRIORITIES	177
49	THE FALLEN	179
EPILOGUE PATH TO NORMALCY		181
AUTHOR BIO		183
EMBRACE THE MYSTERY WEAR THE LEGEND		185
SNEAK PEAK – NIGHT OF THE DOGMAN: THE SCENT		187
SNEAK PEAK – NIGHT OF THE DOGMAN: A STRANGE SIGHTING		191

PRELUDE

THE DELICATE BALANCE

For centuries, the Sasquatch family thrived in the secluded valley of Redmond, California, concealed from the prying eyes of humans. Generation after generation, they upheld their traditions, safeguarding their haven and nurturing their young in the ways of the forest. Now, under the leadership of a wise Patriarch and Matriarch, their existence faced unprecedented challenges.

The Redmond family unit, anchored by the Patriarch and Matriarch, comprised a father, strong and stoic, whose weathered features spoke of years spent navigating the dense forest terrain. Beside him stood the Matriarch, embodying grace and resilience, her keen eyes reflecting a deep understanding of the natural world around her. Together, they formed the steadfast foundation upon which their family thrived.

Their offspring, a pair of siblings, embody the vitality and energy of youth within the Sasquatch community. The elder sibling, a robust male, possesses a boundless curiosity and a fierce determination to explore the mysteries of the forest. His muscular frame and keen instincts make him a natural leader among his peers, while his adventurous spirit often leads him on daring expeditions beyond the safety of their territory.

His younger sister, possessing a sharp intellect and an independent spirit, harbors a heart as untamed as the wilderness itself. With her agile movements and quick wit, she navigates the forest with ease, her infectious laughter echoing through the trees as she chases after butterflies and explores hidden glens. Despite her youth, she possesses a keen intelligence and a fiery spirit that endears her to all who know her.

Together, the siblings formed a dynamic duo, their bond strengthened by shared adventures and the unbreakable ties of family. Whether tracking game through the dense undergrowth or racing through the forest under the silvery glow of the full moon, they faced each challenge with unwavering courage and determination.

As the next generation of the Redmond family, they carried the hopes and dreams of their parents and ancestors, their destinies intertwined with the fate of their Sasquatch community. With each passing day, they grew stronger and more resilient, forging bonds of kinship that would endure the trials of the wild.

From a young age, they were taught the skills necessary to hunt for food, gather resources, and navigate the dense forest terrain. They learned to track prey, identify edible plants, and build shelters to protect themselves from the elements. These lessons were not merely theoretical but were put into practice during hunting expeditions and foraging missions, where mistakes could mean the difference between feast and famine.

Beyond the physical demands of survival, the Sasquatch youth also faced challenges of a more social and emotional nature. As they grew older, they had to navigate the complexities of relationships within their community, learning to resolve conflicts, cooperate with others, and earn the trust and respect of their peers. They grappled with questions of identity and purpose, seeking to find their place within the tribe while also asserting their individuality.

The Sasquatch youth were also confronted with the ever-present threat of human encroachment on their territory as human settlements expanded into the wilderness. Witnessing firsthand the destruction of their habitat and the depletion of natural resources, they were forced to adapt to these changing circumstances. In response, they sought ways to protect themselves and their way of life while also striving for peaceful coexistence with their human neighbors.

Amidst these challenges, a network of aunts, uncles, and cousins extended their kinship, forming a close-knit community of fifty Sasquatches spread across a fifty-mile radius. Each member played a designated role, with their duties intricately woven into the fabric of daily life.

Females, agile and nimble-fingered, gathered plants and berries with gentle care, while sturdy males embarked on hunting expeditions to provide sustenance for their kin. Others were appointed as sentinels, keeping watch in the forest for signs of encroachment or danger.

Like any family, a spectrum of personalities existed among the Sasquatches. Some bore gentle dispositions, fostering harmony within the community, while others harbored a fierce temper, quick to defend their territory against perceived threats.

Periodically, the curiosity of juveniles led them beyond their range, seeking the allure of freedom beyond familiar borders. Occasionally, their wanderings intersected with human activity, prompting decisions fraught with consequence. The Sasquatches faced a dilemma: intimidate intruders to maintain secrecy or deliver swift justice in cases of harm.

Despite efforts to coexist peacefully, tensions simmered beneath the surface. Human settlements encroached steadily, threatening their way of life. For the Sasquatches, the time for a decision loomed ominously. The delicate balance between ancient heritage and the encroaching tide of civilization hung in the balance, shaping the fate of generations to come.

1

HOMECOMING

Jake's hand slammed down on the alarm clock, silencing its persistent beeping as dawn barely broke, the early hour grating against his natural inclination for sleep. Rolling over, he groaned, checking the time. It was 5:00 AM—his vacation back to his hometown of Sutter Creek, nestled in the heart of northern California, was finally here.

Sutter Creek harbored memories both bitter and sweet for Jake. It was where he had grown up, where childhood friendships had blossomed amidst quaint streets and rolling hills. Yet, it was also tinged with the ghosts of his past, memories he had eagerly left behind in pursuit of a brighter future.

As he dragged himself out of bed and began packing his bags, Jake's mind drifted back to his decision to leave Sutter Creek. Determined to escape the confines of small-town existence, he had set his sights on San Francisco, driven by aspirations of becoming involved in law enforcement. It was a dream he had pursued relentlessly, leaving behind haunting memories for the promise of something greater.

After grappling with the decision of pursuing a career in law enforcement, he ultimately opted for the security sector. Years of dedicated study and working low-paying jobs led him to establish his own thriving security firm, which quickly rose to become the top security firm in San Francisco.

Jake's upbringing as an only child in Sutter Creek came with its challenges, particularly with a father who wielded discipline like a heavy-handed ruler and a mother who battled alcoholism, casting a shadow over their household. His mother's death from liver failure when he was just 15 only added to the weight he carried, leaving him to navigate adolescence and family dynamics alone.

Despite the chaos of his upbringing, his best friend Jasper had been a constant presence in Jake's life. Their friendship spanned decades, forged in childhood innocence and strengthened by shared experiences and mutual support.

Jasper's family history was a tapestry of joys and sorrows. Once part of a bustling household, his world was upended when his mother left them behind, leaving Jasper as the de-facto caretaker of their fractured family.

Recently, Jasper had found unexpected happiness in the arms of Tallulah, a vivacious presence whose warmth and kindness captured his heart. Tally, as she was affectionately known, brought a sense of joy and stability to Jasper's life.

Jake's journey back to Sutter Creek held a mixture of anticipation and trepidation. Reuniting with Jasper and revisiting the town that shaped him carried allure but also stirred long-dormant emotions and memories he had sought to bury.

This journey represented a retreat from the turmoil of his life in San Francisco—a deliberate step away from the betrayal that shattered his trust and heart. As he drove through the Californian landscape, the serene beauty contrasted sharply with the turmoil within him.

The past six years with Melissa, once cherished memories, now echoed back as a string of lies. Their love story had ignited unexpectedly, blossoming into a connection Jake believed was once-in-a-lifetime.

However, Melissa's affair with one of Jake's employees shattered their life together. The revelation breached the trust Jake had in her, leading to their separation and Melissa moving in with the person who intruded upon their life together.

In the aftermath, Jake navigated anger, betrayal, sadness, and profound loss. The future they envisioned together crumbled, leaving Jake to sift through the wreckage of a once-solid relationship.

Jake's journey to Sutter Creek was a deliberate retreat, orchestrated alongside Jasper, centered around their shared passion for target shooting. The excursion promised a chance to regain control and clarity amidst life's complexities.

As Jake neared Sutter Creek, his mind drifted to his lodging of choice—the refurbished fire lookout tower, now serving as a secluded retreat. Nestled amidst towering pines, it promised not only adventure and solitude but also breathtaking vistas of Sutter Creek and its surroundings.

Before reaching the tower, Jake had a checklist of errands to tackle, from grabbing essentials to ensuring his Jeep had enough fuel.

Finally arriving at the tower, Jake followed the emailed instructions diligently, punching in the lock-box code to retrieve the keys that awaited inside.

As he approached the base of the lookout, Jake encountered

a six-foot wire fence encircling the perimeter, with a gate serving as the sole entry point. Beyond this initial barrier, a second, heavier gate guarded the base of the tower itself. This secondary gate secured access to the ladder leading up to the lookout—a ladder Jake was about to ascend.

With his backpack securely fastened, Jake made his way through both gates. The physical act of climbing the ladder seemed symbolic, a literal rise above the stress of life below. With a deep breath, he began his ascent, each step up the ladder marking the start of his retreat into seclusion and peace.

The tower's amenities provided for his needs, offering a comfortable stay amidst peaceful surroundings. Its wraparound decking provided unobstructed views of the landscape, immersing Jake in the serene beauty of the area.

As he explored the space, Jake found himself nodding in approval, muttering to himself, *"This is pretty cool."*

Despite minor inconveniences like a camping toilet, Jake knew he made the right choice in accommodation for this trip. As he settled in for the night, he felt thankful for the opportunity to disconnect and recharge amidst the wilderness.

Already looking forward to reuniting with Jasper, Jake sent a text to let him know of his safe arrival. Tonight, however, was about relaxation—enjoying a cold beer as he watched the sunset and indulged in simple pleasures.

With dinner prepared, Jake intended to dive into a good book, letting the narrative carry him away until sleep claimed him. This first night in the tower was about unwinding and easing into the slower pace of life, preparing for the restorative days ahead.

2

NEVER TRUST THE HAIRLESS ONES

As the first light of dawn kissed the treetops, the Sasquatch family stirred from their slumber, ready to embrace the day's tasks.

In the heart of the forest, as the sun climbed higher, casting light on the hidden corners of the forest, the family divided responsibilities with practiced ease.

The females, skilled in the art of foraging, ventured out to gather the day's sustenance—Cattail for its versatility, Salmonberry for a sweet indulgence, and Fireweed, a crucial ingredient for their evening meal. Meanwhile, the males prepared for a day hunt, an age-old ritual essential for the family's survival.

The youngest members of the family, the juveniles, reveled in the freedom of the morning. They chased each other through the dense foliage, their laughter echoing melodiously in the wild. Swinging from tree to tree, they played with unbridled enthusiasm, their youthful exuberance shining brightly in their eyes.

Among them, two young Sasquatches from the Redmond family—a brother and sister—engaged in an energetic game of hiding and finding each other, their spirits unencumbered by the world around them. So absorbed were they in their play that they ventured farther from home than ever before, their curiosity acting as a guiding light.

Their adventure led them to the outskirts of a homestead, a realm entirely foreign to them. The brother, a mix of cautiousness and wonder, crouched low upon spotting a hairless one emerging from a white structure reminiscent of a cave in their primitive minds. His sister joined him, and together, they observed in silence, concealed from view.

The hairless one busied itself with a metallic contraption, its sporadic noises suggesting frustration. Another of its kind, a female, soon appeared, uttering unintelligible words before retreating indoors. To the young Sasquatches, these hairless ones were an endless source of intrigue—a puzzle they yearned to solve. Hours could pass as they observed motionlessly, captivated by the peculiar behaviors and gadgets.

As they watched, hidden amidst the foliage, the wind gently blew in their direction, reassuring them that the hairless ones couldn't detect their scent. This natural shield allowed them to observe closely without fear of being discovered, the young Sasquatches remaining transfixed, straddling the boundary between two worlds.

Despite their fascination, both youngsters remained acutely aware of the stern warnings issued by their elders: never approach the hairless ones, never trust them. These warnings were deeply ingrained in Sasquatch lore, cautionary tales of close encounters and narrow escapes painting the hairless ones as creatures to be wary of.

They were all too familiar with the tragic tale of their father's mother, who had fallen victim to one of the hairless ones many years ago—a poignant reminder of the dangers that lurked beyond their territory. Yet, the innocence and curiosity of youth often blurred the lines of caution, drawing them closer to the unknown.

This day's adventure marked a bold departure from their elders' warnings, driven by an insatiable curiosity, even as they heeded the wisdom to maintain their distance. Despite the warnings, the spirited youngsters couldn't resist the allure of exploration, frequently visiting neighboring homesteads, always observing from a safe distance, their curiosity piqued by the enigmatic activities of the hairless ones.

At times, they even dared to pilfer ripe fruit from trees, their nimble fingers plucking the sweet bounty under the cloak of darkness.

3

A DAY'S ADVENTURE

Jake stirred from a restful sleep, feeling rejuvenated and ready to embrace the day ahead. With eagerness, he climbed out of bed and moved towards the modest kitchenette of his lookout tower accommodation. There, he prepared himself a cup of instant coffee. While it lacked the richness of the brew he savored back home, it was sufficient to kick-start his morning with a much-needed jolt of caffeine.

Stepping out onto the deck with his coffee in hand, Jake was greeted by the morning light that bathed the surrounding tree-tops in a warm, golden hue. The view was breathtaking, with the town visible in the not-too-distant horizon, providing a stark contrast to the endless stretches of forest that surrounded him on all other sides. "Today is going to be a good day," he affirmed to himself, soaking in the beauty of his elevated hideaway.

After a moment of quiet contemplation, Jake decided it was time to set his plans into motion. Retrieving his phone from the bedside table, he dialed Jasper's number, his anticipation growing with each ring. When Jasper answered, a note of excitement was evident in his voice, mirroring Jake's own enthusiasm for the day's activities.

"Hey Jasper, how's it going, man?" Jake greeted him warmly.

"Not too bad," Jasper replied. "I'm totally eager to grab our gear and head out to Coventry Creek Road for some target shooting."

"Yeah, me too," Jake agreed, a surge of anticipation coursing through him. "Alright, give me 30, and I'll be there."

With plans firmly in place, Jake gathered his essentials—a change of clothes, tooth brush, his wallet, keys, and phone—and descended the ladder from his lookout tower. At the base, he took a moment to savor the crisp morning air before making his way to the tower's facilities for a quick shower.

The cold water invigorated his senses, washing away the last vestiges of sleep and leaving him feeling refreshed and alert. Dressed for the day ahead, Jake secured the gates behind him and set off through the town towards Jasper's house, a sense of excitement bubbling within him as he looked forward to the adventures that awaited.

4

COVENTRY CREEK

Jake pulled up to Jasper's place, punctual as ever, greeted by the crisp morning air. Jasper, gear in hand, was ready for the day's outing. Loading Jake's car with various firearms and ammunition, each chosen with care for their target practice, they set out.

While safety was paramount to Jake, always the stickler for proper handling and protocols, Jasper showed a more relaxed approach, occasionally needing reminders of best practices. Jake, ever patient, ensured their preparations were thorough, emphasizing safety above all to balance Jasper's more casual attitude. Their dynamic, a blend of Jake's meticulousness and Jasper's laid-back nature, worked well, keeping their outings both safe and enjoyable.

As they set off towards Coventry Creek Road, the familiar route to their favorite shooting spot, Jake glanced over at Jasper. "How's your dad doing?" he asked, his tone a mix of curiosity and concern. Jasper's father had become somewhat of a recluse, preferring the solitude of their family home ever since Jasper's mother had left them. It was a sensitive topic, but Jake felt it was important to check in on his friend's family, however complicated their situations might be.

"He's keeping to himself, as usual," Jasper replied with a shrug. "But he seems to be doing alright, starting to get out more. Thanks for asking, man."

The conversation shifted to lighter topics as they continued their drive, the familiar landscape rolling past. Their destination was a secluded spot off Coventry Creek Road, known only to a few and cherished by Jake and Jasper for its privacy and the perfect backdrop it offered for a day of shooting.

Upon arrival at Coventry Creek Road, Jake and Jasper wasted no time in setting up their makeshift shooting range. With practiced efficiency, they unloaded their gear from the Jeep and began the familiar routine of preparing their targets. They scouted the area for suitable backdrops and makeshift backboards, selecting sturdy pieces of wood and metal to serve as their shooting surfaces. Working together, they propped up the boards at various distances, strategically placing them to provide a challenging array of targets.

Once the backdrops were in place, they carefully affixed their paper targets, securing them with clips and tape to ensure they wouldn't be blown away by the force of their gunfire. Each target bore a different pattern or silhouette, offering a mix of precision and rapid-fire challenges.

With their range set up to their satisfaction, Jake and Jasper took turns stepping up to the firing line. They methodically loaded their firearms, checking and double-checking the safety mechanisms with the practiced ease of seasoned marksmen. The range of firearms they had brought allowed them to practice with different types of guns, from pistols to rifles, each session interspersed with moments of careful ammunition reloading and safety checks. The sound of gunfire echoed through the open space, a testament to their shared hobby and the skills they had honed over many such outings.

As they focused on their shooting, the outside world faded away, replaced by the rhythmic cadence of their breaths and the steady thud of bullets hitting their targets. For Jake and Jasper, these moments on the shooting range were more than just a hobby; they were a form of meditation, a chance to escape the pressures of everyday life and find contentment in the simplicity of marksmanship.

While preparing his new CZ 457 Jaguar Rifle, Jake turned to Jasper and inquired, "So, how's the bar business going?" His tone conveyed genuine interest in Jasper's venture.

Jasper let out a tired but satisfied sigh. "It's going alright, you know? Keeps me busy, that's for sure. We've got a good crowd most nights. Just trying to keep things fresh and interesting for the regulars."

"That's great to hear, man. You've really turned that place around," Jake commended, knowing how much work Jasper had put into the bar.

"Yeah, thanks. It's been a journey," Jasper acknowledged with a nod.

"And you? How are you holding up after everything with Melissa?" Jasper asked, his voice filled with genuine concern as he glanced at Jake.

The question hung in the air for a moment, a shadow crossing Jake's face at the mention of his ex. He took a deep breath, gathering his thoughts before responding. "It's been tough, not gonna lie," Jake admitted, his voice tinged with a hint of sadness. Jake sighed, running a hand through his hair before turning to face Jasper. "It's just... I don't know if I ever told you, man, but Melissa moved in with the guy she was cheating with," he confessed, the words heavy on his tongue.

Jasper's eyebrows furrowed in sympathy as he processed the revelation. "Damn, man. I'm sorry to hear that," he replied, his voice soft with empathy.

"Yeah," Jake continued, a hint of bitterness creeping into his tone. "And you never realize how much your lives are entwined until you break up. It's like... everything reminds me of her, you know? Places we used to go, things we used to do. It's hard to escape."

Jasper nodded in understanding. "I can't imagine how tough that must be," he said sincerely. "But just remember, you're not alone in this. I've got your back, no matter what."

Jake offered a grateful smile, the weight of his burden momentarily eased by Jasper's unwavering support. "Thanks, man," he said, the words carrying more meaning than he could express. "I appreciate it more than you know."

"Being out here, doing things like this, it helps, you know?" Jake said, looking around. "Keeps my mind off the bad stuff."

Jasper nodded in understanding, his expression sympathetic. "I get it, man," he said softly, his tone laced with empathy. "Sometimes, getting lost in the moment is the best medicine."

A brief silence settled between them, the sound of their breathing mingling with the rustle of the breeze through the trees. Then, Jasper reached out and clapped a reassuring hand on Jake's shoulder, a gesture of solidarity. "Glad to hear you're finding ways to move forward, buddy," he said, offering a supportive smile. "If you ever need to talk or just blow off some steam, you know where to find me."

Jake returned the smile, his gratitude evident in his eyes. "Thanks man," he said, the weight of his troubles momentarily lifted by the warmth of his friend's companionship.

The shooting session then wrapped up, both men feeling a sense of accomplishment and a deeper connection. They had not only hit their targets but also found comfort in each other's company, a reminder of the enduring strength of their friendship. As they packed up, double-checking each piece of equipment and leaving the area pristine, both Jake and Jasper were thankful for the day. It had been a welcome escape, a chance to recharge and reflect on the paths they were navigating.

"Let's head to my bar for a beer and burger," suggested Jasper.

"Oh, hell yeah man," Jake responded eagerly.

They both climbed into Jake's Jeep and set off towards town.

5

THE CHASE

The Sasquatch siblings' peaceful observation of the hairless ones was suddenly interrupted. Sensing a growing unease, the female juvenile signaled her desire to leave by tugging at her brother's arm.

Her brother, however, remained engrossed, muttering they would leave soon. Reluctantly, the female began to withdraw, but as she did, she felt an unsettling shift in the wind—it was now blowing from behind them, carrying their scent directly towards the homestead.

Without warning, a large dog, one of the types that always followed the hairless ones, burst from beneath the structure, charging straight at them. Panic surged through the female, her instincts screaming danger. Reacting instantly, her brother's protective instincts kicked in. He grabbed her, and they bolted, the dog's ferocious barks echoing behind them.

They dashed through the forest, the male leading the way. Despite their swift pace, the female struggled to keep up, her smaller legs pumping as fast as they could. The option to confront the dog loomed over them, an easy but risky choice. It would silence the threat but could draw unwelcome attention to their kind, just as the elders had warned against.

In a split-second decision, the brother veered towards a tree, urging his sister to follow. They climbed higher and higher, confident the branches would support their weight. Below, the dog arrived at the base of the tree, its barks turning into bays as it stared up at them.

Fearing the arrival of a hairless one drawn by the commotion, the siblings knew they had to act fast. They leaped from their perch, moving from tree to tree, a skill they had honed since they could walk. The strategy was to confuse and evade the dog, to lead it away from their trail without resorting to violence.

Their hearts raced as they navigated the canopy, the dog's persistent baying fading and then strengthening as it tried to follow their movements. With each step, the siblings moved with a silent understanding, driven by their desperate desire to return to the safety of their family without incident.

As the minutes stretched, the dog's bays finally began to recede, its presence diminishing as the siblings put distance between them. Eventually, the forest swallowed their figures, the only evidence of their passage the gentle swaying of the trees.

6

A HARROWING TURN

The siblings, breathless yet momentarily safe after resting in a large oak tree, exchanged glances filled with both relief and lingering adrenaline from their flight. The male juvenile's eyes swept their surroundings, a creeping realization dawning on him—they were lost. Their usual markers and familiar trails were nowhere to be seen, replaced by unfamiliar territory that stretched ominously around them. His sister mirrored his confusion, her wide eyes searching for something recognizable in the dense forest.

Their brief disorientation shattered as the sound of a hairless one yelling, punctuated by the relentless barking of the dog, reached their ears. Panic ignited in their eyes, a clear, unspoken decision made between them—they needed to run. Pushing through brambles and bushes that clawed at their hair, they moved with desperate speed, driven by the fear of what might happen if they were cornered.

Suddenly, the female's leg caught on an old, hidden branch, sending her tumbling to the ground with a sharp cry of pain. Without hesitation, the male stopped, turning back to help her to her feet. She pushed past the pain, urging herself to run faster, leading the way in their desperate bid for safety.

Their flight brought them to a sudden, unexpected clearing—the hairless one's path. It appeared suddenly, leaving them little to no time to stop or change course. The male managed to halt at the very edge, but his sister, momentum carrying her forward, emerged directly into the path of a metal beast. The impact was immediate and devastating, the metal beast colliding with the female Sasquatch with a force that crumpled its front end and sent it careening off the road into a ditch.

Frozen by shock, the male Sasquatch's gaze frantically searched until he found his sister, thrown eighty feet from the site of the collision, lying motionless beside the road. Her breathing was shallow, her left side visibly injured and twisted in an unnatural angle. Overcome with fear but driven by an urgent need to protect her, he scooped her up with trembling arms and retreated into the safety of the forest.

Every step was agonized, his mind racing with fear and concern for his sister's life. The young male carried his dying sister for miles, finally recognizing markers to their home. The young male heard a whistle indicating he was coming up on a sentinel Sasquatch, one of the tribe's watchers, stationed to keep guard over their territory and ensure their safety. Upon seeing the young male's burden, the sentinel lifted the injured young female from her brother's arms, carrying her the rest of the way. This act of kindness allowed the brother to lead them swiftly through the underbrush, unencumbered but heavy with worry and sorrow.

As they approached the family's home, the brother's anguished scream echoed through the trees, a chilling herald of the tragedy that had befallen them. His mother, aunt, and the older members of their tribe responded with immediate concern, their hearts heavy with a premonition of despair.

The scene that greeted them was one of profound sorrow. The mother collapsed at the sight of her daughter, the stark finality of her stillness a silent scream that echoed her worst fears. The sentinel gently laid the female's body down, stepping back to allow the family the space to come together in their grief.

The family's mourning was profound, a shared anguish that enveloped them as they gathered around their lost one. The brother, now standing alone, was a figure of desolation amidst the collective grief. Guilt and helplessness consumed him, emotions that were mirrored in the sentinel's solemn demeanor.

As the female Sasquatches tenderly prepared the daughter for her burial, the mother began to hum a haunting melody in their ancient language, her voice carrying the weight of generations of sorrow. Soon, the aunts joined in, their mournful harmonies weaving through the air.

The son sat nearby, lost in a fog of grief and shock. He was painfully aware that his father would soon return, and the knowledge weighed heavily on him, anticipating the fury and disappointment that would be directed at him for not protecting his sister. His thoughts also drifted to the metal beast that had taken her life, fueling a deep anger towards the hairless one responsible for his loss. This mix of dread for his father's reaction and rage against the cause of the tragedy left him feeling trapped in a whirlwind of emotions.

As the melancholic humming filled the air of the camp, it was gradually overtaken by the sounds of the returning male hunting party. The juvenile's heart began to pound with a mix of fear and anticipation, the melody serving as a backdrop to his emotions. He exchanged a glance with his mother, seeing the anguish and concern reflected in her eyes.

The familiar calls of success from the hunters were quickly overshadowed by the heavy, urgent footfalls of his father, who had been alerted to the day's tragic events by one of the sentinels. Upon entering the camp and laying eyes on his daughter's lifeless body in the burial garden, the father was visibly shaken, a wave of devastation washing over him. He glanced towards his partner, finding only shared sorrow in her gaze.

Kneeling beside his daughter, he tenderly touched her cheek with his fingers, whispering softly to her in a final, heartbreaking goodbye. Standing again, he released a scream of anguish that echoed through the forest, a raw expression of pain and loss that resonated with every member of the tribe.

Turning his grief-stricken eyes towards his son, who sat isolated and dreading this moment, the father's sorrow quickly morphed into anger. He strode over, lifting the juvenile to his feet with a firm grip. Harsh vocalizations and grunts of reproach echoed through the forest, the Patriarch expressing his deep disappointment in the juvenile for not safeguarding his sister, signaling for him to reveal the location where his daughter was hurt. Overwhelmed and frightened, the juvenile managed only a soft series of sounds in response, his gestures meekly pointing towards the site of the sorrowful event.

In a surge of blind grief, the father's hand lashed out, striking the juvenile with swift and forceful impact. The blow sent the young one sprawling to the ground, the sheer force of it leaving him stunned and reeling from the physical and emotional pain inflicted by his father's anguish.

The mother, witnessing the harsh discipline, rushed to her son's side, offering comfort as he lay on the ground, trying to grasp the reality of the situation. Amidst the tension, the father commanded the juvenile to lead him and two other male Sasquatches to the location, determined to see the place where his daughter's life had been cut short. The juvenile took one last look back at his sister before setting off with his father and uncles.

7

GOOD COMPANY

As Jake and Jasper pulled up outside The Seedy Greedy Bear Bar, Jasper remarked, "I think Tally's working tonight. You'll finally get to meet her, Jake." Jake responded with a confident smile, "I'm looking forward to it," as they approached the bar. "Anyone who can put up with you so much has to be someone special," Jake added with a playful grin. Jasper chuckled and held the door open, gesturing for Jake to enter first.

Jake was immediately struck by the atmosphere of the place. "Wow," he exclaimed, impressed by the bustling crowd and the seamless blend of modern and rustic decor that Jasper had achieved with the renovation. He gave Jasper a hearty pat on the back. "Well done, man. I'm proud of you!"

Jasper, with a modest nod of appreciation, thanked Jake and suggested he find a table while he sorted something out quickly.

Shortly after Jake sat down, a woman with light brown hair and a radiant smile approached his table. She introduced herself as Tally, his server for the evening, and inquired if he would be dining alone. "No," Jake replied, "I'm here with Jasper. I'm Jake." Tally's eyes widened in surprise, followed by a delighted giggle. She leaned in for a warm hug, expressing her excitement to finally meet him. "I've heard so much about you," she shared warmly. Jake smiled back, sharing kind words in return, and then ordered for both of them—two beers and two burgers.

Tally assured him she'd return shortly with the drinks and left Jake to absorb the lively ambiance of Jasper's bar. Sitting there, he felt a sense of excitement and anticipation, eager to enjoy the evening ahead with good company in a place that clearly reflected his friend's hard work and vision.

8

TREPIDATION

....

The journey through the dense forest was a silent procession of sorrow and trepidation. The young Sasquatch, leading the way, was consumed by feelings of loneliness, fear, and simmering anger. Ahead, the imposing figures of his father and two uncles loomed large, both in physical stature and the weight of their presence.

His father, a giant among giants within their tribe, stood at an awe-inspiring height of nine feet five inches. His broad shoulders and commanding presence marked him as a leader whose very size was a testament to his strength and authority. The uncles, though slightly shorter, shared the familial trait of towering stature, each a formidable presence.

Mindful of the potential dangers from the hairless ones and their vigilant dog, the juvenile chose a circular route to the location. The air around them was heavy with unspoken grief as they moved through the twilight of the forest. The humidity clung to their hair, making the atmosphere thick and oppressive. It was just on the cusp of darkness, the time when the forest begins to whisper secrets of the night.

As they neared the hairless one's path, the young guide signaled that they were close. Without a word, the Patriarch stepped forward, his massive form moving past the juvenile with a determined stride. The uncles followed suit, a silent guard flanking their leader.

Standing at the edge of the forest, the Patriarch paused, his senses heightened as he listened and smelled the air, a ritual of caution before stepping into the exposed vulnerability of the hairless one's path. Once satisfied with the safety, he moved onto the path, his gaze sweeping over the scene with an intensity born of a father's love and anguish.

Drawn to the remnants of the tragedy, he approached the spot where his daughter's blood had spilled—a stark, crimson reminder of the loss they all felt. Crouching down, he sniffed the area, a deep, mournful huff escaping him, a sound that seemed to carry the weight of his sorrow.

The other Sasquatches, standing watch, remained vigilant, their eyes scanning the surroundings. Suddenly, the Patriarch's attention snapped to a moan heard from a short distance across the road. With a mix of curiosity and caution, he rose and moved deliberately towards the source of the noise, signaling for the others to follow.

9

MONSTER

......

Joe's slow return to consciousness was marred by confusion and pain. As his senses gradually sharpened, the stark reality of his situation became horrifyingly clear. He was trapped in the wreckage of his box truck, the cabin twisted and torn around him following the earlier crash.

The cause of the accident flashed back to him—a sudden, shadowy figure darting in front of his vehicle, leaving him no chance to avoid the collision. The impact had sent his truck, loaded with soda drinks, careening off the road and into a ditch before slamming into a tree.

A warm trickle of blood made its way down his forehead, the taste of metal permeating his mouth. Attempting to move, Joe let out an involuntary moan as he discovered his legs were pinned beneath the steering column. The sharp pang of pain forced the air from his lungs, leaving him gasping and momentarily overwhelmed by the urge to close his eyes and retreat from the reality of his injuries. Despite this, the thought of reaching for his phone flickered in his mind, though hope for a signal in this remote area was faint. "I gotta get help somehow," Joe muttered to himself.

In the eerie silence that enveloped the deserted road, heavy footsteps suddenly echoed towards the truck. At first, Joe clung to the hope of rescue, but the absence of any other sounds filled him with unease. The unusual weight behind each step only intensified his growing sense of dread.

Struggling, he managed to locate his phone and activated the flashlight app, desperate for any clarity in the enveloping darkness. Swinging the light towards the passenger window, his heart seized in terror at the sight that greeted him.

Pressed against the glass was a face so grotesque and unworldly it defied logic—a horrific visage that melded human-like traits with those of a monstrous ape.

In the fleeting span of a mere second or two, Joe absorbed the chilling sight before him. The Sasquatch's face, pressed against the glass, seemed to materialize in an instant—a terrifying fusion of human-like features and primal ferocity. Its eyes, deep-set and piercing, gleamed with an otherworldly intensity, reflecting a primal intelligence honed by centuries of survival in the wild. Above them, a broad and furrowed brow furled with concentration, hinting at the creature's formidable strength and cunning.

Beneath the gaze of those red piercing eyes, a broad nose protruded, flared with each ragged breath. Its nostrils, wide and flanked by tufts of coarse hair, twitched with every inhale, detecting scents imperceptible to human senses. The Sasquatch's mouth, framed by a thick and matted beard, curled into a snarl, revealing rows of sharp, yellowed teeth—each one a confirmation of its predatory nature.

As the creature pressed closer to the glass, its features contorted with a mix of hatred and disgust. Deep creases lined its weather-beaten cheeks, etched with the scars of countless battles fought in the unforgiving wilderness. And yet, despite its fearsome appearance, there was a haunting semblance of humanity lingering within those primal eyes.

As fear threatened to overwhelm Joe, the only word that escaped his lips was "Omah," a recognition of the creature's identity dawning upon him.

As Joe's eyes locked onto the creature's piercing gaze, a primal growl erupted from its throat, saturating the air with a menacing intensity that rooted Joe to the spot in fear. Panic surged through him, his heart pounding in his chest like a relentless drumbeat of impending doom. His hands shaking, Joe instinctively reached for the concealed firearm stashed in his truck—a forbidden necessity earned through countless deliveries to dangerous areas.

The moment his fingers wrapped around the weapon, he aimed the flashlight back at the window, only to find the creature had vanished. Doubts of his sanity flickered through his mind, a side effect of his injuries, he wondered.

But then, amidst the stillness, Joe heard the unmistakable sound of multiple sets of feet moving around the truck, their heavy steps crunching on the dirt and leaves. It felt as if they were toying with him, circling in a macabre dance of anticipation. This realization shattered any brief hope he might have harbored. Noise from the driver's side window then intensified his dread, confirming the presence of not just one, but several monstrous beings lurking just beyond sight.

Turning off the safety, Joe pointed the light and gun towards the source of the sound, his body pressed back as far as his trapped legs would allow. A hand, inhuman in its size and appearance, reached through the broken window, gripping his arm. Joe screamed, firing the gun over and over in a blind panic. Each shot was met with an ear-splitting scream from the creature, a sound so close and intense it threatened his hearing.

Suddenly, an excruciating pain erupted in his right shoulder, as if a vice had clamped down on it, dragging him violently towards the passenger side. Agony shot through him like a lightning bolt, radiating from the point of impact and spreading across his entire body. The phone slipped from his grasp, its screen shattering as it hit the floor of the truck, plunging him into darkness once more.

Amidst the chaos, the heavy, ragged breaths of the monster were terrifyingly close, its fetid breath washing over him like a foul gust of wind. His screams were drowned out by the sound of tearing fabric and flesh as the creature's claws shredded through his clothing and sank deep into his skin.

In those final moments, Joe's gaze locked onto the monstrous eyes looming over him, their sinister glow reflecting the pain and terror that consumed him. The world seemed to blur and distort around him as consciousness slipped away, leaving behind only the unbearable weight of unimaginable agony and fear.

10

ECHO'S THROUGH THE FOREST

After silencing the hairless one's screams, the Patriarch Sasquatch circled the metal beast, searching for his son. As he rounded the corner, his eyes landed on a heartrending scene—one of his brothers knelt beside the young Sasquatch, who lay motionless on the ground.

Rushing to his son's side, the father's worst fears were realized. The son had sustained grave injuries from the confrontation, with metal projectiles causing grievous wounds to his face and neck. One had struck his left eye, one had struck him in the back of the throat, and the other had shattered his jaw, leaving the young one without breath, without life.

Overwhelmed by a torrent of frustration, grief, and guilt, the Patriarch let out a harrowing scream that echoed through the forest, a raw expression of the pain of losing his offspring not once, but twice in the same day. This was not merely the loss of his children but the crumbling of future hopes and dreams. He had envisioned his son growing to lead the tribe, a responsibility he had been preparing him for since birth, a future that now lay shattered at his feet.

Witnessing the depth of the Patriarch's despair, the two uncles stepped back to give him space to mourn. The forest itself seemed to hold its breath as the father, consumed by rage and sorrow, unleashed his emotions upon the metal beast. With each blow, the metal groaned and buckled, mirroring the anguish in his heart.

After a few minutes of relentless assault, the Patriarch, his hands bloodied and his body drained from the exertion, finally ceased his onslaught. Taking a moment to catch his breath, he sank to the ground beside his son's lifeless form, the weight of his anguish clear in the stillness of the forest. His heavy breaths mingled with the silence, echoing the depths of his despair.

Watching on with heavy hearts, the uncles understood the magnitude of the Patriarch's pain and guilt. They offered silent support, knowing there was nothing that could ease the burden he bore.

Gently lifting his son's body, the Patriarch embarked on the long journey back to their home, the weight of his loss bearing down on him like an oppressive burden.

Behind him, the uncles followed in mournful reverence, their steps a poignant testament to the sorrow that enveloped them all.

As they traversed the forest, each footfall seemed to echo the collective grief of the Patriarch and each uncle, a mournful procession through a landscape scarred by tragedy. Yet amidst the mourning, a quiet determination simmered within the Patriarch's heart—a steadfast resolve fueled by the fire of vengeance.

Though the tribe would seek comfort and healing together,

the Patriarch's focus remained unyielding, his gaze fixed on a path of retribution.

11

CONSEQUENCES

In the heart of the dense forest, under the canopy of ancient trees, the Sasquatch tribe gathered in a solemn circle. The atmosphere was heavy with sorrow as they prepared for a ritual unheard of in their generations—a double burial for the Patriarch's children.

Their mother was a portrait of despair, her grief evident as she tenderly arranged her offspring for their final rest, her hands shaking with every leaf and branch she placed beside them. Amidst her sorrow, anger simmered, directed at the Patriarch for leading their son into danger, only to return him lifeless.

The community worked together in silence, each movement and gesture steeped in respect and mourning for the lives cut so tragically short. They adorned the burial site with forest blooms and ferns, a natural tribute to the spirits they were returning to the earth.

The Patriarch stood apart from the rest of the tribe. His massive frame was a shadow against the twilight, his face a mask of stoic resignation. Yet, beneath the surface, a storm raged within him. His heart was a furnace of anger, not just for the loss of his children, but for the circumstances that led to their demise.

He knew, deep down, that the Matriarch would never forgive him for their son's death. The weight of her silent accusation hung heavy in the air, a constant reminder of his failure to protect their offspring. Despite his outward appearance of strength, he was consumed by guilt and remorse, haunted by the knowledge that he had led their son into harm's way, with tragic consequences.

As the ritual progressed, the tribe members took turns paying their respects, their low, mournful vocalizations filling the air with a haunting melody of farewell. The mother, overcome with sorrow, was supported by her kin, her cries a stark echo in the quiet of the forest.

The Patriarch, meanwhile, remained silent and unmoving. His eyes, usually filled with the wisdom and strength of leadership, now reflected a void consumed by thoughts of retribution. Inside, he seethed with a rage that burned hotter than any fire. The hairless ones, with their careless ways and metal beasts, had brought this suffering upon his family. In his heart, a vow took root—a promise of vengeance for the irreplaceable lives stolen from him.

As the Patriarch stood alone, the memories of his youth surged forward, a bitter reminder of a past tragedy that mirrored his current despair. Before his offspring had been born, the hairless ones had been responsible for another irreplaceable loss—that of his mother. She had fallen into a pit, cruelly hidden and lined with wooden spikes, a trap set by the hairless ones. Her death had left a deep scar in the heart of their family, a wound that took years to even begin to heal.

His father, the tribe's leader at the time, had counseled against retaliation, warning of the endless cycle of violence it would provoke. He had stressed the importance of preserving their way of life, of focusing on the survival and well-being of their tribe above the pursuit of revenge.

But now, as the Patriarch reflected on the graves of his children, his father's warnings seemed distant echoes, overshadowed by a consuming hatred for the hairless ones. The loss of his offspring, so senseless and violent, reignited the grief and anger of his mother's death, merging past and present into a singular focus of vengeance.

His thoughts were a tumultuous sea, waves of sorrow crashing against the rocks of vengeance. For years, he had lived by the principles his father had taught him, valuing the secrecy and safety of their existence over confrontation. Yet, the repeated transgressions of the hairless ones, culminating in the deaths of his children, had shifted something fundamental within him. The Patriarch felt a visceral need to protect his tribe, not just from the immediate dangers of the forest, but from the ongoing threat posed by the hairless ones.

The forest, usually a place of refuge, now felt like a silent witness to his family's anguish, its peacefulness a stark contrast to the storm raging in his heart.

The Patriarch's determination solidified with the arrival of a fresh breeze, stirring the surrounding foliage and carrying with it a sense of resolve. This time, he vowed, he would not heed his father's warnings. This time, he would let his burning hatred guide him. The hairless ones had stolen too much from him, and they would face the consequences of their actions.

In the quiet of the forest, a plan began to take shape, born from grief, fueled by vengeance. The Patriarch knew the path he chose would change the destiny of his tribe forever. But in the depth of his despair, he saw no other way. The pain of his losses, both past and present, demanded justice. And he would be the instrument of that justice, no matter the cost.

12

SHADOWS OF THE FOREST

"Tally seems like a really nice woman, Jasper. You're definitely on the right track, and I know I said it before, but man, am I proud of you," Jake said, warmth and sincerity lining his words as they sat in the cozy ambiance of Jasper's Bar.

Jasper's smile was genuine, a reflection of his gratitude. "Thanks, Jake. It means a lot coming from you. Taking this on has been stressful at times, but I've got to say, I'm really enjoying the challenge. Tally has been a wonderful partner and incredibly helpful behind the scenes with the bar."

The conversation flowed effortlessly between them, spanning various topics—from memories of past adventures to plans for the future and everything in between. They laughed, reflected, and for a few hours, the weight of the world seemed to lift, replaced by the comfort of old friendship.

As they savored the moment, Jasper's curiosity got the better of him. "Hey, Jake," he began, his voice tentative, "what about your dad? It's been a while since you mentioned him."

Jake's expression faltered for a moment, a flicker of unease crossing his features. "Yeah, it has been a while," he admitted, his voice tinged with nostalgia. "I haven't seen him in over ten years, and it's been six years since we last spoke."

Jasper's eyes softened with empathy as he listened to Jake's words. "Do you think you'll go see him?" he asked gently, his concern evident.

Jake hesitated, his gaze distant as he mulled over Jasper's question. "I've thought about it," he replied slowly, "but I've tried to reach out to him over the years, left messages, but I never got a call back. At this point, I think it's best to let sleeping dogs lie." There was a hint of resignation in his voice, a recognition of the futility of trying to mend a relationship that had long been fractured.

As the evening wore on, Jake glanced at his watch and realized it was time to head back to the watchtower. "I should get going, man. Got to settle in for the night," he said, reluctance tinging his voice, not wanting the night to end but knowing it was necessary.

"Yeah, I get it. Thanks for coming out, Jake. It's been great catching up like this," Jasper responded, standing up to see him out. As they reached the door, Jake turned to Jasper, a thoughtful expression on his face. "I'll give you a call tomorrow night," he said, "We can set a plan for what to do the following day. I know you've got work tomorrow."

"Sounds good man. Have a good night," Jasper replied, and closed the door.

Walking out into the night, the air cool and refreshing, Jake felt a sense of peace. The time spent with Jasper had been a much-needed respite, a reminder of the bonds that grounded him. As he drove back to the watchtower, his mind wandered to the next day's plans. Going into town and taking a leisurely walk around seemed like the perfect way to spend it, especially since Jasper would be busy at work.

The idea of a quiet day to himself was appealing. It would give him time to think, to delve deeper into the familiar corners of the town, and maybe even find a little more peace in the slow rhythm of daily life outside the fast-paced world he was used to in San Francisco. Jake knew that days like these were precious, moments of reflection in the otherwise chaotic flow of life.

Jake arrived back at the watchtower, the familiar creak of the gates echoing in the still night air as he unlocked them both. With a sense of relief, he pushed them open, the hinges protesting softly as they swung wide. The cool night breeze brushed against his skin, carrying with it the scent of pine and earth.

As Jake began to ascend the ladder, his mind wandered. He relished the stillness of the night, the quiet hum of nature surrounding him like a comforting embrace. But then, a sudden noise shattered the stillness—a faint rustling of leaves, coming from the nearby forest.

Pausing in his steps, Jake strained his ears, his heart quickening with apprehension. Was it just the wind, or something else? The night was dark, the moon obscured by heavy clouds, casting the forest in shadows. Squinting into the darkness, he tried to discern the source of the sound, but it remained elusive.

Then, from the shadows of the forest, a figure emerged—a doe, its delicate form illuminated by the faint glow of moonlight filtering through the trees. Jake let out a breath he hadn't realized he was holding, a relieved laugh escaping his lips.

"Guess I'm a bit jumpy after all," Jake chuckled to himself, shaking his head in amusement. *"Too much time in the big city, I've forgotten what it's like to live with wildlife,"* he mused aloud,

the words lost to the night. The doe glanced in his direction for a moment before disappearing into the safety of the woods.

With a wry smile, Jake resumed his climb, ascending the ladder steadily.

Once inside, he settled into bed, enveloped by the calmness of the night and the comfort of a day well spent. The gentle night sounds of the forest whispered through the air, lulling him into a restful state.

13

JUSTICE OR VENGEANCE

Before the first light of dawn pierced the dense canopy of the forest, the Patriarch of the Sasquatch tribe rose from his unrestful slumber. The weight of grief and unresolved anger had kept him awake through the hours of darkness, and as the night began to retreat, he knew the time had come to set his plans into motion.

Gathering the uncles and the eldest members of the tribe in a secluded clearing, he shared with them his intention to seek vengeance against the hairless ones for the deaths of his children. The air grew heavy with tension as he spoke, his voice resolute, leaving no room for doubt or dissent.

The reaction among the gathered Sasquatches was mixed. While some understood the depth of the Patriarch's pain and his need for retribution, others were taken aback, their eyes widening with surprise and concern. There were murmurs of apprehension about the potential consequences of such actions, fears that this path might lead to more suffering and loss for their tribe.

Yet, despite their worries, the respect they held for their leader, coupled with the tradition of unity and obedience within the tribe, silenced any vocal opposition.

Acknowledging their concerns with a nod, the Patriarch requested that a select group of seasoned Sasquatches undertake a crucial mission. He tasked them with seeking out their extended family, spread across neighboring valleys, to enlist their support in the forthcoming confrontation. This was not a request made lightly; reaching out to kin for assistance spoke volumes of the gravity of the situation and the lengths to which the Patriarch was willing to go for his vengeance.

The chosen Sasquatches, experienced and adept at traversing the rugged and untamed wilderness that lay between their home and their extended family's territories, set out at the first light of dawn. Their journey was one of urgency and purpose, driven by the weight of the task at hand and the trust placed in them by their Patriarch and their tribe.

Back in the clearing, the meeting dispersed in solemn silence, each member of the tribe processing the gravity of the decision made. The day ahead would be one of preparation, of sharpening their resolve as they braced for a chapter in their history marked by the quest for justice—or vengeance, depending on the eyes that beheld it.

As the Patriarch stood in contemplation, his resolve as unyielding as the ancient trees surrounding him, one of the tribe's wisest elders approached him. With a voice tempered by years of experience and eyes that had seen the ebb and flow of many seasons, the elder communicated his concerns through a series of expressive grunts and gestures that had been honed into a complex language over generations.

He conveyed a message of caution and foresight, questioning the Patriarch with a solemn depth that resonated through their shared form of communication. His gestures and vocalizations hinted at concerns about the potential risks of pursuing vengeance and whether such actions could be justified.

The elder subtly conveyed their tribe's historical resilience in coexisting with the hairless ones, despite past conflicts and invasions.

With a gentle yet firm tone, communicated through a blend of meaningful pauses and low, rumbling vocalizations, the elder expressed concern that the intense sorrow consuming the Patriarch might be clouding his judgment. This heartfelt exchange emphasized the gravity of the decision, urging a moment of pause and reflection amidst the storm of grief and rage.

The Patriarch, his grief a shield against any doubt, dismissed the elder's concerns. He was unwavering, convinced that the cost of inaction would be higher than the pursuit of retribution.

As the conversation unfolded, one of the Patriarch's brothers observed the Patriarch's stance with a furrowed brow. He had always harbored reservations about the Patriarch's temperament, believing his hot-hotheadedness could lead to further conflict. From his vantage point, he could see the potential consequences of the Patriarch's proposed course of action, and it troubled him deeply.

Despite the Patriarch's conviction, the brother remained unconvinced. He knew that escalating the situation would only sow the seeds of more violence and suffering among their kind. With a worried heart, he hoped that reason would prevail before it was too late.

As his attention shifted from the elder, the Patriarch's gaze fell upon his partner. Her eyes, brimming with profound sadness, met his briefly before she silently turned away. Her departure spoke volumes, a wordless declaration of the growing chasm between them. She believed that enough blood had been split, and vengeance would not bring their offspring back. With a grief-stricken heart, she chose not to participate in his plans, her resolve firm despite the anguish etched upon her face.

Despite the heavy weight of his partner's sadness and the potential rift it could cause, the Patriarch's resolve to pursue vengeance remained unshaken. The understanding and unity he had shared with his partner now hung in the balance, jeopardized by the unwavering path of retribution he was set on. The reflection of grief in her eyes, compounded with a deep-seated fear for the future, did nothing to deter his course.

He felt a compelling duty to show the hairless ones that the Sasquatches had reached their limit. It was time, he believed, to make a stand and show that they would no longer tolerate the intrusion and violence against their family by the hairless ones.

His determination, once a beacon of clear intent, now cast a definitive shadow over his relationships, signaling the inevitable sacrifices that lay ahead. The Patriarch fully grasped the far-reaching implications of his actions, recognizing that the pursuit of vengeance would irrevocably change the dynamics within his tribe and the essence of his connections with loved ones. Yet, this understanding only served to fortify his commitment.

In his heart, the loss of his children had ignited a flame of hatred that no reasoning could extinguish. Yet, amidst his fervor for vengeance, he understood that not all the Sasquatches, particularly the females, would join his plan. He harbored no ill will towards them, recognizing their different perspectives and priorities.

He accepted the looming alterations to his tribe's destiny and the transformation of personal bonds as collateral in his unwavering quest for justice. The depth of a father's fury, coupled with a profound sense of duty to defend his tribe's right to live without fear, justified the forthcoming upheaval. In this crucial moment, he was convinced that demonstrating their strength and resolve to the hairless ones was essential, and nothing—no appeal to reason or emotion—could sway him from the path of vengeance.

14

BRUTAL BATTERING

"What in the hell happened here?" Sheriff Owen demanded, his voice tinged with disbelief as he surveyed the wreckage before him.

"I... I don't know, Sheriff. I don't think the damage happened in the crash," Deputy Reynolds replied, his brow furrowed with confusion.

Together, the two men circled the truck, their eyes widening in astonishment at the extent of the destruction. Every surface bore the marks of a violent encounter, and inside, they discovered Joe Crow's lifeless body, his features unrecognizable beneath the injuries inflicted upon him.

As the Sheriff reached the driver's side, he crouched down, his attention drawn to a dark stain on the ground.

"Do you think that is Crow's blood, sir?" the Deputy inquired.

The Sheriff stood and gazed out into the forest. "I don't

think Joe ever got out of the truck, Deputy."

Without hesitation, Sheriff Owen sprang into action, already coordinating with the county coroner to handle the grim task ahead.

"And who reported this?" Deputy Reynolds inquired.

"Louise, our daytime dispatcher," Sheriff Owen confirmed, his tone carrying a note of familiarity. "She mentioned driving past the wreck earlier this morning and spotting something unusual in the sunlight." His gaze remained fixed on the scene before him, a mixture of concern and determination evident in his expression.

"Deputy, your job is to maintain the integrity of this scene. I'll inform Mrs. Crow of her husband's passing. Ensure thorough documentation, but erase those footprints before anyone else arrives," the Sheriff instructed, pointing out the scattered prints as he walked to his cruiser.

The deputy glanced down, startled to see footprints scattered everywhere, surprised he hadn't noticed them before.

Deputy Reynolds, sensing the gravity of the situation, prioritized the meticulous task of erasing the footprints scattered around the scene. With each sweep of his brush, he worked methodically, ensuring no trace remained for the camera to capture or for the coroner to see upon his arrival.

Once satisfied that the scene was preserved, Deputy Reynolds then turned his attention to documenting every detail with his camera. Armed with his equipment, he approached the wreckage, capturing each twisted angle and jagged edge with precision. Each snapshot served as a haunting reminder of the violence that had transpired in this once-peaceful clearing.

As the shutter clicked, echoing through the silence, Deputy

Reynolds couldn't shake the feeling of unease that lingered in the air. Every detail he captured seemed to hold a piece of the puzzle, a fragment of truth waiting to be unveiled.

Meanwhile, Sheriff Owen had just returned to the station after delivering the grim news to Mrs. Crow about her husband's untimely passing. A solemn atmosphere hung over the station, laden with the weight of serious responsibilities and looming uncertainties. His immediate priority was to debrief Louise on her observations from that morning.

Louise Renlay sat at her desk, her hands trembling as she recounted the events to Sheriff Owen. The morning had taken an unexpected turn for her when she stumbled upon the wreckage, a sight that would linger in her memory for days to come. The unsettling scene had left her shaken, a sense of dread settling over her as she recalled the twisted remnants of the truck.

"I-I just couldn't believe it, Sheriff," Louise began, her voice quivering. "I got out of my car to see if anyone needed help, and… and the damage to the truck, it was like nothing I've ever seen before. Poor Joe Crow, he looked so battered…"

Sheriff Owen nodded, his expression grave as he listened intently. "Go on, Louise. What else did you see?"

Louise took a deep breath, her gaze distant as she recounted the harrowing details. "The weirdest thing, Sheriff, was the footprints. They were bare, too large to be human. I knew I had to get out of there quickly…"

Sheriff Owen's brow furrowed in concern. "Did you see any animals or anyone else around?"

Louise shook her head, her eyes wide with fear. "Animals? No, Sheriff. It was like… like something out of a nightmare. It was really eerie. I-I didn't stick around to find out. I just got back in my car and drove straight here."

The sheriff placed a reassuring hand on Louise's shoulder. "You did the right thing, Louise. Thank you for your bravery. Now, take a moment to collect yourself. We'll get to the bottom of this."

As the sun rose higher in the sky, illuminating the picturesque streets of Sutter Creek, the news of Joe Crow's tragic demise spread swiftly through the tight-knit community. Joe was no stranger to anyone in the small town; he was a familiar face, a friendly presence woven into the fabric of everyday life. His sudden passing sent shock waves through the hearts of all who knew him, casting a shroud of sorrow over the once-bustling streets.

Conversations at local cafes, mom get-togethers, and impromptu gatherings on street corners were dominated by talk of Joe—of his kindness, his generosity, and the senseless tragedy that had befallen him. The news of his death seemed to reverberate through the town, touching each resident in its own way and leaving a profound sense of loss in its wake.

15

SIMPLE PLEASURES

Jake woke up to another day perched high in his watchtower, the sun's early rays casting a soft glow over the treetops. The stillness of the morning, paired with the breathtaking view, offered him a moment of peace before he embarked on his plans for the day. With a leisurely pace set for the day ahead, he decided to venture into town, keen on experiencing its quiet charm under the bright daylight.

The descent from the watchtower was becoming a familiar routine, each step down the ladder reminding him of the unique simplicity his current life offered. Once on the ground, he locked up and made his way towards town, the forest's morning chorus fading behind him as he approached the hum of small-town life.

After finding a parking spot, Jake casually strolled through the shops, unexpectedly bumping into a few old friends. Their chance encounter turned into impromptu catch-ups right there on the sidewalk, each exchange filling Jake with a sense of connection and nostalgia. Despite the time and distance that had separated them, the familiarity of old bonds made their conversations flow easily, reminding Jake of the ties that still anchored him to this place.

One old friend, Mike, excitedly shared recent news. "Hey, man, before you go, did you hear about the sheriff finding a truck that had crashed off the highway last night?" he exclaimed, glancing around warily to ensure no one else was listening. "Yeah, apparently," he continued, "every part of the truck had been smashed in, and they found old Joe Crow crushed in the truck."

"Wow, that's terrible," Jake responded sympathetically.

"Yeah," Mike continued, "ain't no way the truck got damaged like that just running into a ditch. Something or someone else must have done it. If you ask me, it was a Sasquatch."

"A Sasquatch?" Jake repeated, his eyebrows raised in surprise. "You mean like Bigfoot?" Jake asked.

"Yes, exactly," Mike replied with a nod. "There are sightings of them around these parts, believe me."

Jake couldn't help but chuckle at the idea. "Well, that's certainly something," he remarked, still amused by the notion of encountering a mythical creature in the woods.

With that curious conversation lingering in his mind, Jake bid farewell to Mike and continued his stroll through town, his thoughts drifting between the mundane and the mysterious as he soaked in the sights and sounds of the small community.

The town, with its welcoming atmosphere and familiar faces, felt like a different world compared to the isolated serenity of the watchtower. Jake decided to stop at a cozy café he'd noticed the day before. Settling in with a freshly brewed coffee, he enjoyed the warmth of the drink and the buzz of the café. It was the kind of place where time seemed to slow down, allowing him to savor the moment and the simple pleasure of a good cup of coffee.

As Jake sat at his table, enjoying his coffee, he couldn't help but overhear a conversation from a nearby table between two older men. One of them named Ray was recounting sightings of strange ape-like animals around his homestead, mentioning how his dog had chased after two of them just the day before. After a frantic hour of searching, he eventually managed to retrieve his dog.

Curious, the other man named Harvey asked for a description of these creatures. Ray described them as towering creatures, walking and running on two legs, covered in fur or hair, and standing at least 6 to 7 feet tall. They sounded like peculiar apes indeed.

"So, are these critters you've been seeing Bigfoots?" Harvey asked.

"Bigfoots?" Ray replied, his frustration evident. "There ain't no such things as Bigfoots, Harvey!"

"Alright, alright. My pawpaw used to call them 'Boogers' on his property down in Louisiana. They had a hell of a time with them. But if these 'apes' are hanging around your place, Ray, I suggest you start packing your shotgun at all times!" Harvey warned.

"Hah! You might have a point there, Harvey," Ray chuckled.

With that, they changed the subject, leaving behind the debate about mythical creatures and focusing on more practical matters.

Jake found himself amused and intrigued by the conversation but didn't want to let on that he was listening by asking them questions. After paying his bill, he left the café to continue his stroll.

As Jake indulged in some window shopping, the conversation he overheard, coupled with Mike's account of the mangled truck, lingered in his thoughts. The mention of strange ape-like creatures prowling around someone's property stirred a dormant curiosity within him. Though he didn't fully buy into the idea of Bigfoot or any other cryptid, the vivid description painted by the old man certainly piqued his interest.

He couldn't help but wonder if there might be some truth to the tales circulating in the small town. Could there be a rational explanation behind the sightings, perhaps misidentifications of known animals or even elaborate hoaxes? Or was there a remote possibility that something truly mysterious lurked in the depths of the nearby forest?

Despite his skepticism, Jake found himself drawn to the idea of investigating further. After all, he had always been fascinated by tales of the unknown, even if he approached them with a healthy dose of skepticism. With a shrug and a smile, he decided to mention it to Jasper to see if he had seen or heard anything.

Feeling satisfied after a morning of leisurely exploration and unexpected reunions, Jake decided to have lunch at Jasper's bar.

As Jake stepped inside, he was greeted by the warm buzz of the establishment. Ordering a beer and a sandwich, he sank into the cozy ambiance, relishing the sense of fulfillment that washed over him.

It had been a morning well-spent, filled with unexpected reunions and leisurely exploration. As he sat back, taking a sip of his drink, Jake realized that this moment was the most content he had felt in a long time.

Preferring not to disturb Jasper while he worked, Jake savored his lunch alone, the familiar surroundings of the bar providing a comforting backdrop. With the afternoon slipping away, he eventually made his way back to the watchtower, greeted by the calm embrace of the forest.

Before ascending the ladder, he grabbed one of his rifles, figuring its scope would provide a decent substitute for binoculars. After securing it to his back, he climbed up and positioned the rifle within easy reach, planning to take a nap.

Soon enough, Jake drifted off into slumber to the sounds of the forest below.

16

DEFIANCE

....

The afternoon sun filtered through the dense canopy, casting dappled shadows on the forest floor, as anticipation crackled in the air. Summoned to stand united in the face of adversity, Sasquatches from neighboring valleys converged at the designated meeting spot—a secluded clearing known only to those who roamed these ancient woodlands.

Beneath the green canopy, bathed in the warm light filtering through the leaves, the assembled Sasquatches stood tall. Their expressions conveyed a mix of determination and solidarity, each bearing the weight of their shared history and the resolve to confront the challenges ahead. At the forefront stood the Patriarch of the tribe, a towering figure serving as a beacon for those who looked to him for leadership. Beside him stood seasoned Sasquatches who had journeyed to seek aid, now standing with their allies, forming a formidable assembly of strength and purpose.

With deep, resonant vocalizations echoing through the forest, the Patriarch conveyed the gravity of the situation. His words were not mere instructions; they were a declaration, a rallying cry for justice that stirred the hearts of all who listened. The plan unfolded before them: they would advance toward the town on the forest's edge, the domain of the hairless ones who had inflicted untold suffering upon their kind. Tonight, they sought vengeance.

As the Sasquatches absorbed the Patriarch's message, a sense of unity filtered through the air. Each exchange of glances spoke volumes, a silent agreement to stand together in this moment of reckoning. Despite lingering concerns about the potential consequences of their actions, the collective desire for retribution burned fiercely within them. They yearned to make the hairless ones understand the pain they had wrought, to demand accountability for the lives lost to traps, vehicles, and violence.

Enduring in stoic silence for too many moons, the Sasquatches bore the heavy burden of losses and injustices inflicted upon their kin. Fueled by the anguish of the Patriarch's lost offspring, they gathered, unified and resolute, prepared to emerge from their shadowy domain to confront their adversaries head-on.

Amidst the gathering tension, a dissenting voice emerged from the ranks, conveyed in grunts and gestures. It belonged to one of the Patriarch's brother. Stepping forth with deliberate movements, his gaze fixed solely on the Patriarch, he warned of the consequences of the Patriarch's intentions, invoking the echoes of past bloodshed and signaling the peril that lay ahead, not just for their lives but for the very essence of their tribe.

In response, the Patriarch's reaction was immediate and visceral. With a sweep of his hand, he dismissed his brother's concerns, his resolve unyielding in the face of dissent. But the brother, undeterred, stepped closer to the Patriarch, delivering an imposing message: that the deaths of their clan and future generations would be solely on the foolish Patriarch's hands.

Enraged, the Patriarch lunged at his brother, fists clenched and mind consumed by a primal instinct to dominate. Despite being younger and smaller, the brother stood his ground with a resilience born of generations past. Their brutal struggle unfolded, the forest bearing witness to their fight, the sounds of their grunts and the clash of their bodies echoing through the trees.

For what felt like an eternity, they battled, their strength matched only by their stubbornness. Each blow was met with defiance, each strike fueled by a lifetime of pent-up frustration and resentment. Yet, neither seemed willing to yield.

As the struggle wore on, it became clear that one would emerge victorious. With a final burst of energy, the Patriarch delivered a crushing blow, his fist connecting with the brother's jaw with a sickening thud. The brother staggered backward, and with a final forceful strike from the Patriarch, the struggle ended with brutal finality.

Seeing the fallen brother lying there, a few of the Sasquatches moved to retrieve his body, aiming to honor him with a proper farewell. However, the Patriarch grunted, indicating his preference to leave him there for now—a stark display of the consequences of defying his authority. The rest of the tribe remained subdued, their gazes cast downward in acknowledgment of the Patriarch's command.

Though sadness weighed heavily on their hearts, none dared to meet his gaze, aware of the swift and merciless retribution awaiting any challenge to his rule. His unspoken message hung thick in the air, a stern warning echoing through the silent forest.

In the midst of this tense atmosphere, an elder among the Sasquatches stepped forward, his weathered form exuding wisdom and resilience. With deliberate movements, he initiated a reverent ritual for those preparing to embark on the forthcoming battle, bestowing strength upon each warrior.

Gathered in a circle, the Sasquatches bowed their heads in respect as the elder invoked ancient blessings, entreating the spirits of their ancestors for guidance and protection. His chants reverberated through the air, weaving a tapestry of strength and resilience around the warriors.

Each participant felt a surge of energy coursing through their veins, a primal connection to the land and their kin. The elder's words were not just a ceremony; they were a binding oath, a reminder of their duty to uphold the honor of their kind and stand united against their oppressors.

Before departing, the Patriarch Sasquatch bid farewell to his partner in a touching moment tinged with sorrow and uncertainty. Despite his formidable presence as a hunter and fighter, he approached her with tenderness, pressing their heads together in a silent gesture of farewell.

Their bond, forged through countless trials and tribulations, remained unbroken even in the face of adversity. As he turned to walk away, she watched him go, sadness swirling in her heart. While she understood why he needed to go, she didn't entirely agree with it.

As the ritual concluded, a sense of determination settled over the group. With renewed purpose, they moved forward, their resolve unshakable, their spirits fortified by the ancient rites that had bound them together as one.

17

DECEPTIVE PEACE

The Sutter Creek township, unaware of the storm that approached, lay in a deceptive peace. Lights flickered in homes where families settled in for the night, oblivious to the fury that nature itself was about to unleash. Children returned home from their sports practice, their laughter echoing through the streets as they recounted the day's victories and defeats. An older woman sang softly to herself in the kitchen, the aroma of dinner wafting through the house, a labor of love for her husband returning from a long day's work.

The Sutter Creek township lay shrouded in a deceptive peace, unaware of the impending storm on the horizon.

Within the comfort of their homes, families settled in for the night, their minds blissfully ignorant of the impending upheaval about to unfold. Some gathered around the dinner table, sharing stories of their day, while others curled up on the couch watching the tv, seeking the familiar embrace of family.

Meanwhile, the Sasquatches, led by the steadfast Patriarch,

silently advanced towards the township's outskirts. Their eyes gleamed with determination in the moonlight, their hearts pulsating with a singular purpose. Each step brought them closer to their target, their movements synchronized with the rhythm of the night.

This pivotal moment, a clash between two worlds, born from grief and fueled by the primal thirst for justice, hung heavy in the air. The serene night air, once undisturbed, now filled with tension, serving as a tangible prelude to the inevitable conflict that loomed ahead.

As the Sasquatches crept closer, their massive forms moved with an eerie grace, blending seamlessly with the shadows of the forest. Moonbeams danced off their hair, casting an ethereal glow upon their resolute faces.

The once-tranquil forest now hummed with the pulsating energy of imminent conflict. Every rustle of leaves, every whisper of the wind, served as a omen of the inevitable reckoning that would forever alter the dynamic between Sasquatches and the hairless ones.

18

RECKONING

Jake stirred from his nap as the sky painted itself in the colors of dusk, surprised by how long he had drifted off. Shaking off the remnants of sleep, he rose with a stretch, and grabbed a beer before he headed out onto the deck to enjoy the view.

There, in the quietude of his secluded retreat, he had been sinking into relaxation, relishing the peacefulness until an abrupt, resonant whooping sound pierced through the calm. His head snapped towards the north, where the disturbance originated. Even though it sounded distant, its robustness made it clear it wasn't a bird, yet its peculiarity ruled out a human origin. Curiosity piqued, Jake decided he needed a closer look.

Without a moment's hesitation, he ventured back inside to retrieve his rifle, aiming to utilize the scope for a clearer view.

Intrigued by the source of the sound, an inexplicable urge compelled him to maintain a low profile, preserving the secrecy of his presence. Keeping close to the ground, he cautiously retraced his steps, rifle clutched tightly in hand as another whoop echoed from the east.

Despite the fading daylight, there remained sufficient illumination to conduct a meticulous survey of the surrounding forest. Peering through the scope, he scrutinized the dense foliage, his determination waning until a fleeting motion seized his focus.

Pausing to refocus and zoom in, Jake's disbelief mounted at the sight that unfolded before him. *"What the hell are they?"* he whispered to himself, a mix of awe and confusion lacing his voice. There, in a small break among the trees, he could see scores of humanoid figures, their bodies cloaked in hair or fur, advancing in formation. Their path, he realized with a surge of adrenaline, would bring them alarmingly close to the watchtower.

Jake's initial fascination quickly gave way to a growing unease. These were no ordinary creatures of the forest; their size and the deliberateness of their march suggested a purpose and intelligence that was unnerving. As the figures moved, undeterred by the encroaching darkness, Jake understood that whatever these beings were, their presence so near to human habitation, and their sheer numbers could only spell trouble.

While Jake observed the advancing figures, a profound sense of dread enveloped him. His heart pounded fiercely, his hands beginning to shake with the onset of fear. *"They can't possibly be what I think they are,"* he murmured to himself, the realization too unbelievable to fully accept.

Peering through a gap in the decking, Jake noted the diverse characteristics of the creatures. Some were dark brown, their hair blending seamlessly with the shadows; others were chestnut or blonde in color, their sturdy frames moving with determined purpose. Their varying heights and widths adding to the eerie spectacle unfolding before him.

Feeling a sense of overwhelming danger, he quickly ducked down, making himself as small as possible, desperate not to be detected.

As Jake listened to their heavy footsteps drawing nearer, a whirlwind of thoughts raced through his mind. *What are they doing here? Where are they going? Why are there so many?* Questions swirled, each one adding to his mounting apprehension.

The sudden halt of the Sasquatches only intensified his curiosity, their congregation near the tower raising even more questions. And at the heart of it all stood the towering figure, unmistakably their leader, casting a formidable presence that sent a chill down Jake's spine.

From his concealed vantage point, Jake watched, transfixed and horrified, as this leader communicated with the group—not only through commanding gestures and powerful chest-beating but also via a series of chatters. The chattering was primal, possibly a language, but entirely beyond Jake's comprehension. It added an eerie layer of complexity to the creature, highlighting its intelligence and social structure.

Then, in a moment that would haunt Jake for years to come, the leader let out a bone-chilling cry, a sound so primal and forceful it cut through the night, silencing the forest. To Jake, it sounded unmistakably like a declaration of war, a rallying call to the Sasquatches that filled the night with a noticeable tension. Hiding with his heart racing, Jake realized the gravity of the situation unfolding before him.

Despite not being a praying man, Jake found himself silently pleading that the Sasquatches hadn't detected him, fearing they might attempt to ascend the ladder to his hiding spot. As the large Sasquatch signaled the others to run, a surge of panic shot through him. They sprinted with alarming speed, a wave of fury hurtling towards the unsuspecting town.

"*I've got to warn the townsfolk, I've got to warn Jasper,*" he thought urgently.

19

CALL EVERYBODY

With the Sasquatches edging closer to town, Jake knew he had only moments to act. Crawling with stealth and haste, he reached for his phone, his heart pounding in his chest. The thunderous pounding of their footsteps grew ominously closer, driving him to move even faster.

Holding his breath, Jake sat motionless, a silent witness to the storm of creatures racing towards an unsuspecting town, the weight of their potential arrival pressing down on him with a terrifying force.

Jake positioned himself half on the bed, shrouded by the blanket to ensure no light from his cell phone could betray his location. His fingers fumbled for Jasper's number in the darkness, the urgency of the situation making his heart race. As the call connected, Jake braced himself for the conversation ahead.

"Jasper, you have to listen to me," Jake started, his voice almost a whisper and trembling with a mixture of desperation and fear. "I know this is going to sound crazy, but you have to believe me. There's a tribe of Bigfoots or Sasquatches—whatever they're called—heading straight for town. I'm talking about forty of them, maybe even more, and they're coming fast."

On the other end of the line, Jasper's response was tinged with disbelief. "Bigfoots, Jake? Have you been drinking or something, buddy?" Jasper laughed.

"No, man, I'm dead serious!" Jake insisted, his voice tinged with urgency. "I was just waking up from a nap, sitting out on the deck, enjoying the peace, you know? Then, out of nowhere, these bizarre, loud whooping sounds startled me. That's what drove me to check things out. And through my rifle scope, Jasper, I saw them as clear as day. I couldn't believe my eyes! They had gathered right beneath the watchtower before they took off running—a whole bunch of them. I couldn't even keep count, but they're heading straight towards town."

Jasper was skeptical. "This has got to be a joke, or maybe some prank, Jake. Bigfoot isn't real! You sure they weren't bears or heck, some kids pulling a fast one in monkey costumes?"

"When have I ever been one to pull pranks, Jasper?" Jake countered, frustration seeping into his tone. "And when have you ever seen forty bears together in the woods, huh? I'm telling you, I saw them with my own eyes. They were enormous, covered in hair, with faces so grotesque you'd have nightmares. And they were communicating in some language I couldn't make out. Those were no people, Jasper, not by a long shot."

Jake tried to moderate his voice, aware of the need for stealth. "You need to call the sheriff, warn everyone. I can't say why they're all riled up and headed for town, but it's definitely not for anything good."

The silence that followed was thick with skepticism. Jasper, though a good friend, found the tale too far-fetched to accept without question. "Jake, Bigfoots? That's the stuff of legend, not reality."

"I wouldn't be calling you if I wasn't absolutely sure," Jake pressed on, the fear evident in his voice. "I know it sounds crazy, but it's true. You need to warn the town. Call the sheriff, heck, call everyone! Do something. We don't have much time."

There was a heavy sigh from Jasper, the sound of a man wrestling with the implausible reality presented to him. "Okay, Jake," he finally conceded, albeit reluctantly. "I'll call the sheriff, but I'm doing this because it's you asking. You understand if he laughs me off the phone, right?"

"Thank you, Jasper," Jake said, a weight lifting slightly off his shoulders with Jasper's reluctant agreement. "Just please hurry."

"I will, Jake," Jasper replied, a note of seriousness cutting through his skepticism. "But I'm going to be pissed if this turns out to be some elaborate prank."

"I understand," Jake assured him, the urgency in his voice underscoring the gravity of the situation. "Just trust me, Jasper. Lives might depend on it."

20

LAY OFF THE HAPPY JUICE

After ending the call, Jake lay back under his blanket, the dim light of his phone screen fading as he clicked it off. The silence that enveloped him was now filled with a new tension, a waiting game for what would come next. Had he done enough to avert disaster? Would Jasper's call to the sheriff prompt any action, or would it be dismissed as a prank?

Jake knew that if he was still having a hard time believing what he saw, Jasper would have a hard time convincing the sheriff too.

Jasper's mind raced as he contemplated what to say, his finger hesitantly dialing the sheriff's number. With each ring, his apprehension grew, echoing through the silence until Sheriff Owens' familiar voice finally broke through, answering the call.

"Sheriff, it's uh... Jasper Bosher. I... I know this is going to sound crazy, but I got a call from my buddy Jake about... uh, a group of Bigfoot heading towards town," Jasper stumbled through his explanation, his voice tinged with hesitancy.

There was a pause on the line, followed by a burst of laughter. "Jasper, you almost had me there! Bigfoot? Really? What is this, some kind of joke?" Sheriff Owens managed to say between chuckles.

"No, Sheriff, I'm serious. Jake saw them," Jasper insisted, urgency in his voice. "He was pretty shaken up. Said there's about forty of them heading towards town from the south." Jasper paused, emphasizing his next words. "And let me tell you, Jake's not a man who lies. If he says he saw something, then you can believe he really did, even if it sounds ludicrous."

The sheriff's laughter ceased abruptly, replaced by a serious tone. "Jasper, I know Bigfoot are real, but forty of them sounds a little far-fetched. I wasn't sure if you were just pulling my leg, but I've known you and Jake since you were in diapers, and I can't see you lying about this. So, just in case there is a bunch of Bigfoot coming for town, I'll call in some off-duty deputies. I will tell them I've got word of some teens causing mischief and to keep an eye on it. But Jasper, we need to handle this quietly, otherwise, the townsfolk will panic."

Jasper was taken aback, his confusion evident in his voice. "Wait, what? Did you say you believe in Bigfoot, Sheriff?"

"Yes, Jasper," the sheriff responded calmly. "Although, I prefer to call them Sasquatch. I've seen them a few times outside of town when I've been hunting. They usually leave us be, so that's why I find it hard to believe they are advancing on our town."

Jasper was in shock, his mind struggling to comprehend the implications of the sheriff's revelation.

"Uh... okay, Sheriff. I will empty the bar and tell everyone to go home. Thanks." Jasper hung up the phone.

21

MOMENT OF RECKONING

Jake found himself staring at the ceiling, caught between the urge to hide and the moral obligation to intervene. A part of him yearned to remain concealed, seeking refuge within the watchtower's confines as chaos loomed on the horizon.

Yet, deep within his core, he recognized that remaining passive was not an option. The weight of responsibility pressed heavily upon him as he grappled with the magnitude of what he had witnessed. The imminent danger was undeniable, swiftly encroaching with every passing moment. His mind raced with questions, pondering the effectiveness of his potential actions. Could he descend the ladder and rush into town to warn the residents? But against such a formidable adversary, what difference could one man make?

As Jake deliberated, his phone erupted with a call from Jasper. The tension in Jasper's voice reverberated through the receiver, conveying a sense of urgency.

"Jake, you won't believe it, but the Sheriff is convinced about

Bigfoot. He's seen them while hunting," Jasper relayed.

"Really?" Jake's voice betrayed his disbelief. "Will he take action?"

Jasper confirmed, "Yeah, he's not sold on the idea of forty of them, but he's dispatching off-duty deputies for a patrol."

"Well, that's a relief. Thanks for the update, Jasper," Jake acknowledged.

Jasper continued, "I'm clearing out the bar, Jake. It's safer that way."

"Good call," Jake agreed. "I'll join you soon. I'll check for any lingering Sasquatches before descending the ladder."

"Alright, just watch your back," Jasper cautioned.

"I will. You too," Jake affirmed.

After ending the call, Jake lay on the bed, straining to detect any lingering sounds of Sasquatch activity. With silence prevailing, he cautiously ventured onto the decking, keeping low as he surveyed the surroundings for signs of danger.

Satisfied that the coast was clear, he steeled himself for action. Grabbing his rifle, phone, and keys, he descended the ladder, hoping he could reach Jasper in time.

22

BUCK OUT OF LUCK

....

Buckley Jones slammed the flimsy back door behind him for the fifth time this week. Remarkably, despite its precarious hold on the hinges, the door remained intact. Known to the townsfolk simply as Buck, he was a figure more often avoided than approached, his temperamental nature and penchant for trouble leaving many wary of crossing his path.

The source of today's argument with his wife was a familiar one—Buck's relentless drinking, which had now devoured the last remnants of their government assistance check. With a cigarette dangling between his fingers, Buck sought respite in the haze of smoke, eager to distance himself from the incessant nagging of his wife. This brief escape into the nicotine cloud offered a momentary reprieve from the escalating strife that had, yet again, engulfed his home.

Mumbling to himself about the perpetual misfortunes of his life, Buck lamented how everything, including life itself, had always been crap to him. He railed against his wife, branding her a 'miserable old sod' under his breath. In his embittered monologue, Buck's words were laced with venom and defeat, a reflection of a life marred by regret and misplaced anger.

He settled into the worn chair on his porch, the cigarette smoke curling lazily around him. As he brooded over his misfortunes, a twig snapped in the forest behind his home, shattering the eerie silence of the night. Buck's head snapped up, his senses on high alert.

With his false bravado, he called out, "Who's there?" His voice wavered slightly, betraying the underlying fear that churned within him. When no reply came, he rose from his seat, the adrenaline coursing through his veins.

"Show yourselves!" he bellowed, his voice echoing into the darkness. "I'm armed, and I ain't afraid to use it!" But the forest remained silent, its secrets cloaked in shadow.

After a tense moment, Buck hesitated, his bravado waning in the face of the unknown. With a nervous glance over his shoulder, he retreated back to his chair, the sense of foreboding lingering in the air around him.

Buck's mumbling ceased abruptly when he noticed the eerie quiet around him. This silence, profound and unsettling, lacked the usual cacophony of insects—a stark absence that made it seem as if nature itself had recoiled in anticipation of what was to come.

Deep in the pit of his stomach, Buck knew something wasn't right and suddenly felt immense dread. He had neglected to switch on the porch light upon stepping out, relying instead on the moonlight that typically bathed his backyard..

Then, from right behind him came a growl so deep and menacing it seemed to echo from the depths of a nightmare. The sound, imbued with an evil intent, was enough to still Buck's heart. He could feel the hot breath of whatever was growling. Paralyzed with fear, he could not muster the courage to turn and face the source of the sound.

A sense of unease gnawed at Buck's insides, an intuitive warning that something was terribly wrong, blossoming into a suffocating dread. Overwhelmed by terror, Buck felt a warm liquid spreading over his jeans.

In that moment of utter fear, Buck—a man defined by a life of hardship and anger—found himself whispering prayers into the encroaching darkness, desperately seeking salvation from the looming threat.

Yet, no divine intervention came to Buck's aid. The Sasquatch, fueled by primal rage, executed a swift and brutal judgment. With terrifying ease, the creature placed each of its hands on the sides of Buck's head. In one swift, brutal motion, it tore his head clean off and hurled it against the side of the house—a gruesome testament to the creature's immense strength.

This act of savagery marked the end of Buck's turbulent journey, a life extinguished as suddenly as it had been lived.

Meanwhile, inside their home, Vera's startled voice pierced the chaos. "What was that racket, Buck?" she called out, unaware of the horror unfolding just beyond their door.

Hearing Vera's voice, the enraged Sasquatch redirected its malevolent fury towards the house. It crashed through the back door with unbridled force, shattering the once-peaceful night with a cacophony of destruction and terror. Thus began a nightmare that would soon engulf the entire town, its residents caught in a relentless tide of violence and fear.

23

HARROWING SYMPHONY

In the dimly lit warmth of The Seedy Greedy Bear Bar, Jasper's heart pounded against his chest as he made a split-second decision that would disrupt the calm of the evening. He rushed towards the fire alarm mounted on the wall, his resolve hardened by Jake's urgent warning. Without hesitation, he pulled the alarm, the shrill sound piercing through the bar's usual hum of conversation and laughter.

As the alarm blared, confusion and panic spread among the patrons like wildfire. Jasper wasted no time, jumping onto the bar to make himself heard over the chaos. "Everyone, listen up! You need to get out, now! Head straight home, and stay safe!" His voice carried a weight of authority that few had seen from him, compelling those gathered to heed his warning despite their bewildered protests. "If you haven't finished your meals or drinks, come back tomorrow and they will be on the house. We apologize," Jasper announced.

The urgency in Jasper's eyes left no room for doubt, and the patrons and staff, though confused, began filing out of the bar, the alarm's warning echoing in their ears. Amidst the scramble, Jasper spotted Tally, his girlfriend, trying to calm some of the more panicked customers. Grabbing her hand, he pulled her close. "Stay with me, Tally," he said, his voice a mix of fear and determination. "It's not safe. We've got to stick together."

Tally, sensing the gravity of the situation from Jasper's tone, nodded, her trust in him absolute.

After ensuring the bar was emptied and all his employees were safely ushered out, Jasper moved with purpose behind the bar. He retrieved his gun, a precaution he never thought he'd need to use under such circumstances. With Tally by his side, he stepped outside into the night, his protective instinct in full drive.

The street, usually alive with the sounds of nightlife, was eerily deserted. A few patrons were hastily making their way to their cars or walking briskly down the block, eager to heed Jasper's unexpected call for an immediate evacuation. The blaring alarm had ceased, leaving behind an unsettling silence that seemed to amplify the smallest of noises—a distant car door slamming shut, the soft scuffle of hurried footsteps fading into the distance.

As they stood there, under the dim glow of the street lamps, Jasper allowed himself a moment to doubt. The empty, quiet street in front of him made it hard to believe in the imminent danger that Jake had warned them about. Could it be that Jake had been mistaken? That there was no tribe of Bigfoot creatures about to descend upon their town?

But as the thought crossed his mind, the night air was shattered by a sound that froze Jasper and Tally in their tracks—in the distance a loud woman's scream piercing the night, filled with terror and urgency. Almost immediately, it was echoed by more screams, a chorus of fear and panic that heralded an imminent danger. In that moment, Jasper knew he had been terribly wrong to doubt. The threat was real.

With no time to waste, Jasper gripped the gun tighter and looked to Tally, whose face mirrored his own fear and determination. "We need to find a safe place to hide," he whispered, the urgency clear in his voice.

24

LEAVING THE WATCHTOWER

With screams in the distance, Jake's resolve hardened despite the fear coursing through his veins. He couldn't, in good conscience, remain perched in the safety of his watchtower while his friend could be in trouble.

Jake hastily descended the ladder, each step bringing him closer to the unfolding nightmare below. Despite the metallic coldness of the ladder, a fierce determination burned within him. He was acutely aware of the danger awaiting him, but the thought of standing idly by while others potentially perished was inconceivable.

Reaching the ground, Jake wasted no time unlocking the gates and sprinting towards his Jeep. His hands, though shaking, were guided by purpose as he unlocked the vehicle.

But before sliding into the driver's seat, he made a crucial stop at the trunk. There, he retrieved two bags filled with an array of guns and laid them on the passenger seat. From one of the bags, he pulled out his 12-gauge shotgun—a weapon he never imagined using against a threat like Sasquatch—placing it within easy reach if needed.

He turned the key in the ignition, the engine roaring to life, breaking the silence that had settled over the immediate area. The headlights cut through the darkness as he drove towards town, the familiar roads now seeming alien under the night sky.

25

FUTILE RESISTANCE

Deputy Sam Murphy sat in his patrol car, enjoying a chicken, lettuce, tomato, and mayo foot long sandwich his wife had packed for him before his shift. The familiar streets of Sutter Creek passed by, the deputy navigating effortlessly through the town he knew like the back of his hand.

Sutter Creek wasn't known for its crime rate, so Murphy thought it was just him on duty tonight, with the Sheriff on call if needed. Typical incidents involved drunk drivers from the local bars or minor domestic disputes—nothing too serious, which suited Murphy just fine.

Eva Ford, the night dispatcher, manned the desk, passing the time watching reruns of "Friends" during the quiet night shifts.

At 34, Murphy was looking forward to the arrival of his second child in a few months, grateful that his job didn't bring him too much stress.

As Murphy rounded the corner of Rickards Lane and Main Street, his radio crackled to life. "Deputy Murphy, come in," Eva's voice sounded through the radio.

"What's up, Eva?" Murphy responded.

"The phone lines are going crazy with reports from the south of town about some weird-looking bears," Eva relayed, her voice urgent. "Marjorie Thompson also reported hearing smashing windows and screams. Can you check it out?"

"Sure thing," Murphy replied confidently. "Mark me as on my way," he added as he set his sandwich down on the seat next to him.

"Will do," Eva replied. "Something must be going on because the Sheriff requested Deputies Foggarty and Chang to sign on for patrol too," she continued.

"Sounds like it," Murphy replied. "Over."

Murphy flicked on his lights but left the siren off—there wasn't much traffic in this small town. Approaching Wilson Road, he slowed down, catching sight of something darting across the road at an alarming speed. *It was too swift for a human; maybe it was a bear? We only have black bears up here, but what else could it be*, he wondered to himself.

As Murphy approached the area where the creature had disappeared between two houses, he slowed the patrol car to a crawl, scanning the surroundings intently. Despite his thorough search, there was no sign of it. Perplexed by the creature's sudden disappearance, he continued on his patrol route. Finally, pulling up to Marjorie Thompson's house, he parked at the curb and stepped out of the patrol car.

The night seemed unusually quiet as he scanned his surroundings. Suddenly, a scream pierced the silence, causing Murphy to instinctively reach for his weapon. With a vague idea of the scream's origin, he moved cautiously, keeping an eye out for anything out of the ordinary.

Deputy Murphy strode down the path leading to Mrs. Thompson's home, flanked by rows of lush rose bushes on either side. It was evident that gardening was a cherished pastime for Mrs. Thompson, the pride of her home apparent in the meticulously tended foliage.

As Murphy ascended the porch steps, a sudden explosion shattered the stillness of the night. The front door burst open, and before he could react, a towering beast, at least nine feet tall, barreled out, crashing into Deputy Murphy and hurling him into the thorny embrace of the rose bushes. Stunned and ensnared by the prickly foliage, Murphy cried out in pain, struggling to disentangle himself. *"What the hell was that?"* he muttered.

With a creeping sense of dread, he lifted his gaze, his eyes meeting the nightmarish sight before him. Towering above him was a creature beyond comprehension—a monstrous apparition, its enormity casting a shadow over Murphy's rapidly escalating terror.

Even in the dimness of the night, devoid of streetlamp illumination, the beast's hideous form was unmistakable. And in its monstrous jaws, it gnawed with grotesque relish, its attention fixed on its grisly meal—a severed arm, still clad in a white sweater, a macabre indication as to the horror that had befallen Marjorie Thompson.

Frozen in terror, Murphy's mind reeled, grappling with the inconceivable reality before him. All coherent thought evaporated, replaced by a primal instinct to survive. Frantically scanning his surroundings, he searched for his weapon, only to realize it had been lost in the chaotic upheaval moments before. As he scooted backward on his hands and knees, Murphy met the creature's unblinking gaze.

With lumbering steps, the beast advanced toward him, its colossal frame casting an ominous shadow over Murphy's quivering form. Frantically, he protested, his voice a desperate plea in the night.

"No, no, no!" he yelled, pushing himself away from the approaching creature, but his cries would go unanswered.

The Sasquatch lifted its foot and stomped down onto Deputy Murphy's chest with a deafening crunch, each bone-shattering blow echoing the final, agonized cries of the deputy as the darkness of oblivion took over him.

The Sasquatch, sated on its grisly feast, lumbered away into the night, leaving behind the shattered remnants of Deputy Murphy's futile resistance.

26

PATH OF DESTRUCTION

As Jake reached the outskirts of town, the devastation before him was stark. Houses appeared ransacked, and bodies were visible on front porches and steps, evidence of the path of destruction left by the Sasquatches. The scene was a grim deviation from the town he knew. Each street he passed looked different; some eerily quiet, while others showcased people futilely trying to outrun the rampaging creatures.

As he drove, Jake's every sense was heightened, his grip on the steering wheel tight with anticipation. The cool night air was punctuated by screams and roars, adding to the foreboding atmosphere that gripped the town. Nothing could brace him for the harrowing experiences that lay just moments ahead.

Jake turned onto Main Street, a Sasquatch charged at the Jeep, its sheer force shaking the vehicle as it collided with the side. The impact was deafening, metal groaning under the creature's strength. Jake's heart raced as he fought to maintain control, realizing he was in a battle for his life.

With the Jeep still moving, Jake didn't hesitate. He quickly put the passenger window down, took aim with his 12-gauge shotgun, and fired at the Sasquatch now running alongside the vehicle. The sound of the shot echoed through the streets. The creature let out a pained roar and slowly fell behind.

Jake sped up, putting distance between himself and the injured Sasquatch, but his relief was short-lived. He could see multiple Sasquatches running between houses and crossing the road in a blind rage, forcing Jake to swerve and dodge, each maneuver more desperate than the last.

He realized that the town had become a battleground, and he was right in the middle of it. With each passing moment, Jake's resolve was tested. He couldn't outrun them forever; the Jeep wouldn't withstand another direct attack. His mind raced for solutions, for how he could safely get to Jasper's bar.

As he navigated the chaotic streets, his focus remained on survival. The weight of his shotgun provided a small comfort, a reminder that he wasn't entirely defenseless. But the devastation he saw and the number of Sasquatches made it increasingly clear that they were not merely wandering through the town—they were hunting.

Drips of sweat fell down Jake's face as the Jeep careened through the darkened streets, its headlights casting long shadows that danced menacingly along the abandoned facades of the town. Just as he thought he might have evaded the immediate danger, a Sasquatch stepped out directly in front of the vehicle with startling suddenness. Jake's reflexes kicked in, but it was too late. The Jeep crashed into the creature, triggering the airbags with a thunderous pop. The impact sent a shock wave through the vehicle, jolting Jake against his seatbelt with bruising force.

The Sasquatch, caught in the glare of the headlights, was

thrown to the side of the road, its massive form crumpling under the force of the collision. For a moment, everything was eerily silent, save for the hissing of the Jeep's engine and Jake's labored breathing.

Knowing the Jeep was no longer an option and understanding the gravity of his vulnerability, Jake acted swiftly. Glancing at the Sasquatch lying on the side of the road, writhing in pain, he felt a surge of urgency to put as much distance between himself and the creature as possible. With two bags filled with guns and ammunition and his trusted 12-gauge shotgun in hand, he made a dash for a back alley behind a row of stores. His heart hammered in his chest as he ran, his head on a swivel looking for any sign of danger.

Finding a concealed spot amidst the refuse and shadows, Jake hunkered down to catch his breath. The alley provided a momentary respite from the direct threat, but the sounds that filled the night air were enough to keep his adrenaline surging. He could hear the unmistakable sound of Sasquatches running through the streets, their heavy footsteps a constant reminder of the danger lurking just beyond his hideout.

Mixed with the creatures' movements were the screams of townspeople, a chorus of terror that painted a vivid picture of the nightmare unfolding in the heart of the town. The sound of windows breaking, structures being torn apart, and the continued roars of the Sasquatches created a tune of destruction, the likes of which Jake had never imagined he'd witness.

Hidden in the shadows, Jake tried to steady his racing heart, gripping his shotgun tightly as he weighed his next move. The town was under siege, and every moment he remained hidden was a moment lost in getting to Jasper. Yet, rushing out into the open without a plan was tantamount to suicide.

Jake took a few moments to assess his surroundings, tracing mental maps of the town's layout and estimating the distance to Jasper's bar. Knowing the path would help him navigate strategically, avoiding as many Sasquatches as possible.

27

SEEK SHELTER

Jasper and Tally, their hearts racing with a mix of fear and adrenaline, found themselves crouched in the small, cramped space of the bar's cellar. The decision to hide there had been made in haste, a desperate attempt to seek shelter from the nightmare that had descended upon their town. The cellar door, barely noticeable under the bar counter, seemed like a safe place to hold out until Jake arrived.

The darkness surrounded them, a thick blanket of silence wrapping around their hiding spot. They held their breaths, listening to the chaos unfolding outside. The distant screams and the sound of destruction were a constant reminder of the terror that roamed the streets.

Then, abruptly, the noise drew closer. The unmistakable sound of the bar's back door being forced open sent a shiver down their spines. The heavy, deliberate footsteps that followed reverberated through the cellar, each step a thunderous beat in the quiet hideaway. Jasper and Tally exchanged a look, their eyes wide with fear, as the realization set in that a Sasquatch had entered the bar.

They could hear it moving around, the sounds of furniture being tossed aside and glass shattering filling the air above them. The creature was searching, hunting for any sign of the hairless ones it sought to destroy. Its breathing, a deep and guttural rasp, echoed down into the cellar, so close that Jasper and Tally felt as if the creature was breathing down their necks.

Tally's hand found Jasper's in the darkness, gripping it tightly as if to anchor herself to some sense of safety. They dared not make a sound, barely even breathing, for fear of drawing the Sasquatch's attention. The minutes stretched on, each second an eternity as they waited, prayed, and hoped that the creature would leave without discovering their hiding place.

The Sasquatch's footsteps eventually began to move away, its search taking it further into the bar. They could hear the clatter of pots and containers being tossed aside, the creature feasting on whatever it pleased. Then, mercifully, the sounds moved towards the broken door, and finally, after what seemed liked hours, the creature exited.

Jasper and Tally remained in their hiding spot, too afraid to move, listening intently for any sign that it might return. As the sounds of its departure faded, the silence that followed was almost more terrifying. They were alone again, but the fear of what waited outside the cellar door kept them paralyzed.

The town they loved, the life they had built, was crumbling around them, and in that small, dark cellar, Jasper and Tally faced the harrowing reality of their situation.

28

IT'S THE END

....

Dusty wiped the grease off his hands, squinting in the dim light of his garage. The '68 Mustang, a relic from his late uncle, lay before him, its engine open like a patient on an operating table. As he tinkered with the motor, the quiet of the evening was shattered by distant yelling and screams.

Curious, Dusty stepped out onto his driveway, peering down the street. At the end, a figure emerged, running toward him with wild eyes and frantic movements. It was Sheriff Jackson, a respected figure in the town. But something was off about him tonight. His clothes were torn, streaks of blood splattered across his shirt, and his eyes were bloodshot and wild.

As the sheriff passed, he shouted, "It's the end! Save yourself!" Dusty couldn't help but notice that as the sheriff ran, he kept turning to look behind him, as if he was being pursued by some unseen terror.

Perplexed and unnerved by the sheriff's behavior, Dusty watched him disappear down the street. His heart raced with concern. Sheriff Jackson had always been a pillar of the community, steady and reliable. Seeing him like this sent a chill down Dusty's spine.

Shaking off the encounter as best he could, Dusty retreated back into the safety of his garage, closing the door behind him. But the unease lingered, casting a shadow over his thoughts as he resumed his work on the Mustang. Something was definitely wrong in town, and Dusty couldn't shake the feeling that it was only the beginning.

As he strolled into his backyard, a blood-curdling scream pierced the night, causing his heart to skip a beat. He looked toward the source, only to see his neighbor, Gary, frantically trying to climb over the fence. Before Dusty could react, Gary was violently pulled back, his screams abruptly silenced.

Fear gripped Dusty's heart as he spun on his heel, intent on returning to the sanctuary of his home. But before he could take a step, an earth-shattering crash echoed through the air. He whirled around to see the backyard fence splinter and buckle under the force of an immense creature.

Frozen in terror, Dusty watched in horror as the monstrous form burst through the wreckage, its eyes gleaming with pure hatred. With a surge of adrenaline, Dusty turned and fled, his heart pounding in his ears.

But the Sasquatch was faster.

With thundering footsteps, it closed the gap between them, its hot breath ghosting over Dusty's neck. In a desperate bid for survival, Dusty screamed and sprinted, but it was futile.

With a brutal shove, the Sasquatch sent him sprawling hard to the ground, the wind knocked out of him. Gasping for air, Dusty barely had a moment to comprehend his fate before the creature's massive foot descended upon his back with crushing force.

Pain exploded through Dusty's body as the weight of the beast crushed his bones, the world fading into darkness as death claimed him.

29

HAUNTING SYMPHONY OF SUFFERING

The area south of town was in absolute chaos. Homes lay in ruins, families torn apart, and frantic individuals darted in every direction, desperate for safety. Amidst the pandemonium, one man stumbled upon an abandoned police cruiser. With the keys still in the ignition, he seized the opportunity and raced away, the urgency of escape pulsing through his veins.

As he careened around the corner, panic seized him, his heart pounding in his chest. In his frantic attempt to navigate the tight turn, he misjudged the distance and slammed into the back of an SUV. The impact wasn't enough to trigger the airbags, but it sent a shock wave of fear through him.

Frantically, he shifted into reverse, trying to extricate himself from the collision. But as he put the car in drive, a sudden, unimaginable force yanked him violently from the driver's seat, his body propelled through the shattered window. The world spun in a blur around him as he was torn from the safety of the vehicle, even as it continued its forward trajectory, the engine's roar melding with the mayhem unfolding around him.

Terror gripped the man as he felt himself lose control, his bowels releasing in sheer horror as he stared into the eyes of his attacker. His final thought was of the putrid stench emanating from the Sasquatch's breath, searing into his senses before his world plunged into eternal darkness.

Two streets over, a woman frantically tried to flee on a small scooter. Her heart pounded in her chest as she navigated through the debris-strewn streets, her only thought to escape the nightmare that had engulfed her once-peaceful town. With every twist of the throttle, she pushed the scooter to its limits, the engine whining in protest against the weight of her fear.

As she rounded a corner, a deafening roar shattered the air, her heart leaping into her mouth. Before she could react, a colossal figure lunged from the shadows, blocking her path with its massive form. The woman put her foot down and swerved sharply, attempting to evade her pursuer, but it was too late.

In a swift and brutal motion, the Sasquatch reached out, its massive hand closing around her, lifting her effortlessly from the scooter. She screamed as she felt herself lifted into the air, her desperate struggles futile against the creature's overwhelming strength. With a guttural growl, the Sasquatch dragged her into a backyard, disappearing into the darkness with its helpless prey.

In the aftermath, all that remained was the echo of her screams.

Just east of her location, two men careened down the street in their battered pickup truck, their faces flushed with adrenaline and alcohol. Armed to the teeth with shotguns and fueled by liquid courage, they started firing through their open windows, their shouts of defiance drowned out by the thunderous blasts of their guns. Bullets tore through the air, finding their mark every now and then as the Sasquatches scattered in disarray.

Bob and Reggie were notorious brothers who seemed to spend more time on the wrong side of the law than the right. Returning to town after a hunting trip, they were met with a scene of anarchy and destruction as Sasquatches ran rampant, leaving death and devastation in their wake.

Incensed by the sight of their town under siege, Bob and Reggie threw caution to the wind, driven by a reckless determination to rid their streets of the monstrous invaders. Rationality and self-preservation were cast aside in favor of blind confidence, as they embarked on a perilous mission to take back their town.

For a fleeting moment, it appeared they might escape, Reggie's urgent cries urging Bob to push the truck harder. But then Bob noticed something amiss—the truck was slowing down despite his efforts to accelerate. Frantically, he glanced down and saw an empty beer can wedged under the accelerator pedal.

As Bob struggled to dislodge the can, the Sasquatches closed the distance with frightening speed. Reggie's shouts of encouragement turned to panicked screams as the massive creatures bore down on them, their fury unleashed upon the helpless truck.

In a frenzied onslaught of claws and teeth, the Sasquatches tore through the truck's defenses with terrifying ease. Bob, paralyzed by fear, felt a searing agony as a hairy arm reached through the shattered window, its monstrous grip locking around him like a vise. With brutal force, the Sasquatch hoisted him up, tearing his limbs from his body in a sickening display of raw power, leaving him writhing in unimaginable torment.

Amidst Bob's piercing screams, he found himself locked in a chilling stare with his assailants, their evil red eyes boring into his soul with a ferocity that froze him to the core. But the horror was far from over. As Bob lay gasping for breath, his world spinning in agony and blood loss, a Sasquatch seized his leg, swinging him mercilessly against the unforgiving metal of the truck, each bone-breaking impact driving him closer to the brink of oblivion.

Meanwhile, another of the monstrous creatures turned its attention to Reggie, wrenching him from the safety of the car and hurling him with brutal force into a nearby brick wall. The sickening crunch of bone and the agonized screams filled the air as Reggie's spine snapped and his skull fractured under the relentless assault. With methodical precision, the Sasquatch approached Reggie, its grasp tightening around his head until his skull yielded with a sickening crack, creating a vivid scene of unfathomable terror.

Their once-bold bravado shattered by the merciless onslaught, the hunters now lay broken and defeated, their bodies twisted and maimed beyond recognition. Their screams of pain echoed through the night, a haunting symphony of suffering. nity, steady and reliable. Seeing him like this sent a chill down Dusty's spine.

30

HUNTED AGAINST THE HUNTER

Jake had finally regained his breath when suddenly the piercing cry of a police siren shattered the night, a sound both alien and familiar in the desolate soundscape. His heart leapt with a fragile hope, the possibility of rescue igniting a spark in the oppressive gloom.

Peering cautiously, yet desperately, from his cover, Jake's eyes landed on the spectacle of a police car barreling down the road with reckless abandon. The driver's side door had been savagely torn off, and smeared with a telling crimson. As the car careened out of control, crashing into a nearby yard with a jarring thud, the sight extinguished Jake's fleeting hope, plunging him back into the harsh reality of his predicament.

The silence that followed the crash was heavy. Jake's mind raced, the initial shock giving way to a primal urge for survival. The crashed police car, may have a working radio, he thought. Yet, approaching it meant exposure, risking a confrontation with the unknown forces that had reduced the town to this state of siege.

With the stakes higher than ever, Jake made his decision. The need to survive, to continue fighting against the odds, propelled him forward. His movements were calculated, a delicate ballet of stealth and speed as he navigated the treacherous path towards the wreckage. Each shadow, each noise, set his nerves on edge, the anticipation of discovery a constant companion.

As he drew closer, the remnants of the police car loomed like a monument to the fall of mankind's order. Jake's eyes scoured the surroundings, his senses on high alert for any sign of the Sasquatches.

Reaching the car, Jake's search became frenzied, driven by the dual engines of fear and necessity. His hands trembled as he reached for the radio to find it in ruins.

It was then, in the thick of his desperation, that a sound froze him to his core—a low, guttural growl, ominously close behind him. Jake's blood turned to ice, the realization hitting him with the force of a freight train: he was not alone. The Sasquatch had been drawn by the crash, or perhaps by Jake himself.

In that moment, time seemed to stand still, the night air charged with the electric tension of a hunter and its prey. Jake knew that his next actions would determine his fate, in a dance as old as time—the hunted against the hunter, with survival hanging precariously in the balance.

31

A DANCE WITH DEATH

With his heart racing and the growl of the Sasquatch filling the air, Jake knew he had mere seconds to act. Adrenaline surged through him as he turned to face the looming shadow. In a desperate bid for survival, he aimed his weapon and fired, the shot striking the Sasquatch's hip.

The creature let out a roar, not only of pain but of sheer fury, as Jake dashed for cover behind the wrecked police car. His mind raced, knowing that brute force wouldn't be enough to stop such a formidable creature. As the Sasquatch advanced, Jake's survival instincts kicked in. He remembered the layout of the streets, the nearby yards, and the dense foliage that could offer concealment.

With the Sasquatch closing in, Jake made a bold move. He darted from his hiding spot and led the creature on a harrowing chase through the maze of abandoned cars and overgrown gardens. The beast, enraged and relentless, pursued Jake with terrifying speed, but Jake's knowledge of the area and smaller, more agile size, gave him a crucial advantage.

In a moment of calculated risk, Jake led the Sasquatch into a narrow alleyway, its exit blocked by debris. The creature, driven by instinct and anger, followed, its massive form barely fitting between the walls. Jake, pressing himself into a shadowed recess, held his breath as the beast passed by, mere inches away.

As the Sasquatch realized the trap it had fallen into, Jake seized the moment. With the creature momentarily distracted, struggling to turn its massive body in the confined space, Jake emerged from his hiding spot.

Utilizing the environment to his advantage, he leaped out and fired at the Sasquatch's face, causing the right side of it to disintegrate in a gruesome spectacle. Instead of a roar, the creature emitted a gurgled whining sound.

Not content to wait for the Sasquatch to succumb, Jake fired again, this time aiming for its neck. The Sasquatch staggered, falling to its knees as it clutched its wounded neck, before ultimately collapsing forward. Jake, anticipating the potential arrival of more Sasquatches drawn by the shotgun blasts, wasted no time. He dashed into the adjacent yard, seeking cover amidst a dense bush.

After what felt like an eternity hiding in the shadows, Jake knew he couldn't stay concealed forever. The sounds of destruction had ebbed somewhat, granting him a false sense of security as he made the decision to move. Clutching his 12-gauge tightly and his bag of guns, he emerged from his hiding place, a back alley behind a row of battered storefronts.

Jake moved cautiously, sticking close to the walls and shadows, his senses on high alert. The weight of the shotgun in his hands was both a comfort and a grim reminder of the reality he faced. Every shadow seemed to move, every noise a potential threat. Despite his fear, Jake pressed on, driven by a need to find Jasper, to do something—anything—in the face of this nightmare.

As he rounded a corner, his heart leaped into his throat. A Sasquatch, massive and imposing, stood directly in his path, its back momentarily turned to him. The creature's sheer size was staggering. It turned, sensing his presence, and their eyes met—a moment suspended in time, predator and prey.

Instinct took over. Jake raised his shotgun and fired. The first shot hit the creature in the shoulder, but it barely faltered, letting out a roar of pain and anger. Jake pumped the shotgun and fired again, backing away as he did. The Sasquatch advanced, undeterred, a living nightmare bearing down on him.

The narrow alleyway left little room to maneuver, each step backward a dance with death. Jake fired a third time, a lucky shot through the right cheek that finally brought the beast down.

The silence that followed was deafening, broken only by Jake's labored breathing and the distant sounds of the reckoning.

He had barely made it out alive. Looming over the fallen Sasquatch, Jake felt a mix of relief and sorrow.

Recovering from the harrowing encounter, Jake pressed forward cautiously, sticking to the protective cover of the shadows. With only two streets separating him from the bar where he hoped to find Jasper, every step was a calculated risk. His head swiveled constantly, alert to any movement in the eerie silence that enveloped the town. Aware that the blasts from his shotgun could attract more Sasquatches, he quickened his pace, eager to avoid further confrontation.

Every sound made him tense, but his determination to reunite with Jasper fueled his resolve, propelling him swiftly through the deserted streets. The thought of encountering more of the creatures filled him with dread, yet he knew retreat was not an option. The oppressive silence, punctuated only by his own footsteps and sporadic screams, intensified the night's terror.

As the neon glow of the bar's sign flickered in the distance, Jake's anxiety surged. Amidst the chaos engulfing their town, the prospect of finding refuge with Jasper and others offered a glimmer of hope. His heart raced with anticipation as he approached, his focus laser-sharp—reach the bar, locate Jasper, and strategize their next move.

However, his determination wavered as he caught sight of a lone shoe, incongruously abandoned and protruding from a nearby bush of a nearby house.

32

UNIMAGINABLE HORROR

In the town's east, Caleb and his friends lounged on bean bags and sofas, their attention fixed on the latest horror movie on Netflix. His parents had gone out for dinner, leaving him and his friends some money for pizza. It was a typical scene for a Friday night, a group of teenagers enjoying a scare-fest in the comfort of Caleb's home.

As the horror movie played out on the screen, bloodcurdling screams seemed to reverberate through the room, setting nerves on edge. Unease crept in among them, gnawing at their excitement.

"Hey, Caleb, can you turn it down a bit?" one of the girls asked, her voice quivering with apprehension.

Caleb nodded, reaching for the remote to lower the volume. But to their horror, as he adjusted the settings, the screams only seemed to grow louder, drowning out their attempts to silence it.

"What the hell!," one teen girl exclaimed.

Perplexed, Lyle approached the front window to investigate. As he peered outside, his eyes widened in shock, and a guttural scream tore from his throat.

"What is it? What's wrong?" Caleb and the others cried out, their pulses racing.

With trembling hands, Lyle pointed toward the driveway, his voice choked with terror. "There's... there's something out there... something freaking huge!"

Before anyone could react, the front door exploded inward with a deafening crash, and a massive beast burst into the room, its eyes blazing with feral hunger. Anarchy erupted as the teens scrambled to escape the onslaught, but the creature's ferocity was unmatched.

The once-welcoming space descended into unimaginable horror. Desperate attempts to flee were met with the relentless onslaught of the monstrous intruder. Limbs flailed, screams pierced the air, and the sickening sound of flesh being torn filled the room.

Derrek, seizing his iPhone, aimed the camera at the rampaging beast, hoping to capture its terrifying glory. But before he could hit record, the Sasquatch surged forward, its jaws closing around Derrek's face in a brutal grip.

A gut-wrenching scream echoed through the room as the teen's horrified friends looked on in shock and disbelief.

In a matter of seconds, the Sasquatch tore away flesh and bone, leaving nothing but a bloody, mangled mess in its wake. The smartphone fell to the ground, its screen cracked and splattered with blood, the recording capturing only the confusion and carnage of the savage attack.

Angie, Caleb's 18-year-old girlfriend, was gripped by such overwhelming fear that she bolted straight through the sliding glass door leading to the patio, heedless of the danger. With a sickening crash, the door shattered, sending large shards of glass raining down around her. In her desperate flight, she was impaled by a jagged fragment that tore through her chest with a fatal blow. She collapsed on the deck, her life slipping away in a harrowing mix of gasps and gurgles.

Caleb's heart pounded in his chest as he backed away from the Sasquatch, his mind struggling to comprehend the nightmare unfolding before him. With each passing second, the realization sank in that they were hopelessly outmatched, trapped in a deadly game with a creature of unfathomable strength.

In a desperate bid for survival, Caleb's gaze darted around the room, searching for any means of escape. Spotting the knife block in the nearby kitchen, he lunged forward and grabbed a large knife, his hands trembling with fear and adrenaline. Screaming, he charged at the creature, his mind consumed by a singular thought: to fight for his life.

But his courageous attempt was met with a deafening roar from the Sasquatch, its massive frame towering over him, even smashing out a ceiling light. With lightning speed, the beast lashed out, its powerful foot connecting with Caleb's chest with bone-crushing force. A searing pain shot through him as he was propelled backward, crashing into the garage door with a sickening thud.

Agony engulfed Caleb as he slumped to the floor, blood gushing from his mouth, his ribs shattered and piercing his lungs. Darkness swirled at the edges of his vision as he struggled to draw breath, his consciousness slipping away with each passing moment.

Through a haze of pain and confusion, Caleb barely registered the Sasquatch's approach, its looming figure casting a shadow over him. With a final, guttural growl, the creature raised its massive clawed hand, poised to deliver the fatal blow.

And then, everything went black.

33

DON'T MAKE A SOUND

Pushing aside the branches, Jake discovered a small girl, about seven years old, her eyes wide with fear and confusion. She was huddled in the bush, her body covered in blood that wasn't her own.

"Hey, it's okay. You're safe now," he said, extending a hand. Her response was a whisper, "Rai."

Rai's introduction was brief, her name the only information she offered, but her eyes told a story of loss and terror that words could never capture. Jake pieced together the likely scenario—her family had probably fallen victim to the Sasquatches. The realization filled him with a protective fervor.

"Stay right next to me, and don't make a sound," he instructed her, his tone gentle yet firm. Rai nodded, her small hand finding his in the darkness. Together, they moved through the shadows, Jake's eyes scanning for any sign of the creatures that had turned their world upside down.

The journey to the bar was a stealth mission, every sound and movement magnified in Jake's heightened state of awareness. The weight of his responsibility for Rai added a layer of determination.

As Jake and Rai rounded the corner onto the street where the bar was located, his heart sank. Three Sasquatches were there, their distinct chattering filling the air as they loomed ominously in the parking lot across from the bar. The sight of them, so close to his destination, sent a wave of dread through him. But engaging them was not an option; the risk was too high, especially now with the responsibility of Rai.

With a quick assessment of the situation, Jake decided they would take the back alley, hoping for a more discreet entrance into the bar. He paused at the alley's entrance, scanning for any signs of danger. When he felt confident it was clear, he motioned to Rai to run fast down the alleyway, his focus sharp, aware of every shadow and sound.

Reaching the back of the bar, Jake's fears were confirmed— the door had been violently removed from its hinges. Jake paused at the threshold of the bar, the weight of the moment settling on his shoulders. Beside him, Rai's presence was a quiet reminder of the stakes at hand.

Taking a deep breath to steady his nerves, he prepared himself for the multitude of scenarios that might unfold within those familiar, yet now potentially foreboding, walls—destruction, mayhem, or worst of all, the lifeless body of his friend Jasper.

Moving slowly, with every sense on high alert, Jake entered the bar, Rai by his side. The dim light filtered through broken windows, casting long, eerie shadows that danced across the floor. His eyes darted around, swiftly taking in the scene of disarray: overturned chairs, shattered glass, and debris that littered the interior. Each step was measured, cautious, as he navigated through the chaos, acutely aware of Rai's small form keeping pace with him, her trust implicit in her silence.

Jake's heart pounded in his chest, each beat a loud echo in the quiet space as he and Rai moved further inside, searching for any sign of Jasper or Tally.

With each step, Jake's apprehension grew, a knot of fear tightening in his stomach. The possibility of encountering a Sasquatch within the confined space of the bar was a terrifying prospect. The thought of finding his friends harmed—or worse—weighed heavily on him, a burden shared silently by the young companion at his side.

"Jasper? Jasper, are you here?" Jake whispered with urgency, his voice just loud enough to carry over the silence without alerting any nearby Sasquatches. He tread carefully, avoiding the broken tables and chairs, navigating through the debris and broken glass that littered the floor. Rai, mirroring his cautious steps, remained a silent shadow, her eyes wide and vigilant.

As he rounded the bar, a soft, cautious voice broke the silence. "Jake, is that you?" The relief in Jake's heart was unmistakable as he watched the cellar door inch open slowly. Jasper's familiar face peeked out from the darkness, a surge of relief visible in his eyes upon seeing Jake—and noticing the small figure by his side.

Without hesitation, Jake rushed towards them, a mixture of excitement and profound relief washing over him. "I'm so glad to see you, man," he breathed out, his voice heavy with emotion. Jasper emerged from the cellar, closely followed by Tally.

They all came together in a tight embrace, a moment of solace amidst the chaos. It was then that Tally, pulling away slightly, noticed Rai standing close to Jake. With a curious tilt of her head, she asked, "Who's this?"

Jake took a deep breath, the story of their meeting spilling out in a few quick sentences. He explained how he found Rai, alone and frightened, with evidence of a tragedy but no words to describe it. Tally listened intently, her expression softening with each word.

After he finished, she bent down to Rai's level, offering the young girl a warm, reassuring hug. The simple gesture spoke volumes, weaving Rai into the fabric of their small, makeshift family with an unspoken promise of protection and care.

Jake's voice cut through the heavy silence, his tone tinged with urgency. "Jasper, is there a room we can go talk in? I feel vulnerable out here in the main room of the bar, especially when the Sasquatches could come in at any second."

34

AS CRAZY AS IT SOUNDS

ristan Frias, an 11-year-old boy, enjoyed his nightly ritual of gazing at the stars from his bedroom window before bed. His family's quaint home in the north of town was quiet; his parents had retired to bed just moments ago. However, his peaceful moment was abruptly interrupted by an odd sound emanating from a neighboring property.

Tristan's senses heightened as he scanned the area, his curiosity high by the unfamiliar noise. His gaze locked onto a large creature, moving swiftly on all fours toward the back door of the neighboring house. Shock washed over him as he witnessed the door shatter under the force of the creature's assault. The air filled with screams and sounds of furniture being torn apart. A gunshot pierced the commotion, leaving behind an eerie silence that hung heavy in the night air.

Just then, his mother burst into the room, having heard the noises next door. She hurriedly instructed Tristan to hide in his "cave" and not to emerge until she or his father came to get him.

With trembling hands, Tristan dashed to the closet, pulled back the loose wood, and crawled into his makeshift hideaway. Once a quiet place for reading with his flashlight, now he prayed it would shield him from whatever evil lurked outside until his parents found him.

As silence swept over the house, Tristan's fear intensified. Suddenly he heard the front window shatter, sending glass flying everywhere. A deafening shotgun blast followed, accompanied by his mother's screams. Through the pandemonium, he heard his father's desperate cries urging his mother to run, then another shotgun blast. Terrified, Tristan strained to hear as footsteps thundered up the stairs, his heart racing with dread, tears streaming down his cheeks.

The footsteps approached his room, and Tristan's fear reached a crescendo. However, relief flooded over him as his mother's face appeared, moving aside the wood to reveal his hiding place. She pulled him into her arms, and together they descended to the basement, where his father awaited.

Locking the basement door and barricading it with furniture, the Frias family huddled together, clinging to each other in a desperate bid for safety, hoping and praying that this nightmare would soon come to an end.

"Dad," Tristan whispered, his voice shaking with fear, "what was that thing?"

His father's expression was grave as he replied, "I don't know for sure, son. But as crazy as it sounds, I think it was a Bigfoot."

35

THE PLAN

A s Jake, Jasper, Tally, and Rai gathered in the back office room, Jake spoke to them softly: "The Sasquatches are outside in the parking lot, and no doubt more are lurking around," he began, each word carrying the weight of their dire situation. As he recounted his journey through the town, the details painted a grim picture of a community ravaged. "They have entered just about every home, ransacked them, attacking the families and destroying everything in their wake.

Jasper, visibly shaken by the confirmation of the horror outside, finally spoke. "I'm sorry, Jake. When you first told me, it... it just seemed too bizarre to be true." He ran a hand through his hair, a gesture of stress long familiar to his friends. "But seeing this, knowing they're right outside... It's hard to wrap my head around it. Our town, overrun by Sasquatches."

Jake responded with a reassuring tone, "It's okay, man. I wouldn't have believed my own story either. But what's more important now is that we come up with a plan," he declared firmly. "I managed to grab two bags full of guns and ammunition, but we can't just go out there and start shooting blindly. Once the Sasquatches hear gunfire, they'll swarm us from all directions."

Feeling thirsty, Jasper grabbed some bottles of water from his mini-fridge beside his desk and handed them out. "Okay, Jake. What's the plan?" he asked.

"We go to the roof," Jake declared, his voice firm with resolve. "We have plenty of guns and ammunition. The Sasquatches can't reach us up there. Unless the sheriff managed to alert the surrounding counties, we have to assume that help won't be coming anytime soon. Our best bet is to hold out until sunrise. From the roof, we can barricade the door and fend off any Sasquatches that come along the road."

Tally, her brow furrowed with concern, voiced her apprehension. "What about the decking on the second level? They can climb that, surely?"

"I doubt it," Jasper replied, his tone tinged with uncertainty. "It's off-limits to people because of its age. I don't think it would hold their weight."

With a unanimous nod of agreement, they realized their fate teetered on a knife's edge. They couldn't risk the possibility of the Sasquatches reentering the bar and discovering them. Therefore, taking refuge on the roof appeared to be their best shot at survival and putting an end to the onslaught ravaging their town.

As they ascended the stairs and reached the third floor, Jasper's urgent tone cut through the tension. "We'll need to go through the attic room to get to the door that leads out onto the roof," he declared. "It doubles as a storage room with old furniture in it. We could use that to block off the stairs and buy ourselves some time."

"Sounds good," Jake responded, stepping into the room. Together, Jake, Tally, and Jasper began stacking furniture down the stairs while Rai looked on.

Among the old chairs and tables, Jake's discovery brought a mix of surprise and frustration. "Are you kidding me?" he exclaimed, pointing to an old piano tucked away in the corner.

Jasper, intrigued, joined Jake in clearing the clutter. "How the hell did anyone ever get this up here?" he wondered aloud. "I never even knew it was here."

"We'll have to find a way to get it down the stairs quietly," Jake said, contemplating the challenge ahead. "If we just push it, it's going to make a racket, and those Sasquatches will come running. Maybe if we lower it down slowly, one step at a time..."

Jasper nodded in agreement. "That might work. We'll need to be careful though, and make sure it doesn't slip or make too much noise."

With cautious determination, they devised a plan.

With makeshift ropes and pulleys, they meticulously lowered the piano down the stairs, inch by inch, taking care to muffle any sounds with cushions and blankets. Though it was slow and painstaking work, they persevered until the piano was safely positioned against the rest of the furniture blocking the stairway, all without alerting the nearby Sasquatches.

Satisfied with their efforts, they shut the door to the roof behind them, securing it with a solid wood block. "That's the best we can do for now," Jake remarked, a note of grim determination in his voice.

As Jake surveyed the perimeter, scanning for any sign of the encroaching Sasquatches, Jasper, Tally, and Rai took a moment to gather themselves. Rai, clinging to Tally's side, seemed haunted by unseen terrors, and Tally felt a sense of responsibility to comfort the traumatized girl as best she could.

Meanwhile, Jake's gaze shifted to the aging decking below, its weathered boards offering a precarious footing. The structural integrity seemed dubious at best, with missing sections and signs of decay evident from years of neglect. He wondered if even a slight disturbance from a mouse would send the entire platform crashing down.

Jake looked up as the sound of an approaching vehicle caught his attention, its engine roaring as it sped down the street. It was a minivan, hurtling past the bar at full speed, heading south. Despite the blur of motion, Jake could discern that the vehicle was packed with people. He offered a silent prayer for their safety as they raced away from the danger lurking in the town.

As screams pierced the air, originating from the buildings behind the bar, Jake's senses sharpened. He could feel the impending threat of the Sasquatches drawing closer, their presence casting a foreboding shadow over the area. A furrow formed on his brow as he noticed smoke billowing from a row of houses in the distance, a grim indication of the turmoil unfolding throughout the town.

"Tally, do you know how to handle a gun?" Jake asked as he approached the bags of weapons and ammunition. Tally's response was swift and confident. "You mustn't know me well yet, Jake," she retorted. "I've been hunting all my life and know my way around guns."

"Great," Jake replied, a glimmer of relief in his eyes. "Grab whatever you need from these bags and make sure you're well stocked on ammunition." Turning to Jasper, he added, "And you too, grab what you need before the Sasquatches arrive. We need to be ready."

Jake swiftly selected his weapons of choice, opting for the .300 Winchester Magnum rifle. With a Smith & Wesson's six-shot .44 Magnum tucked into his waistband as a backup, he felt a surge of confidence coursing through him.

Jasper wasted no time in making his selection, opting for the .308 Winchester Magnum rifle, a reliable firearm with a proven track record. He also grabbed the 1911 Range Officer® Elite Operator® 10mm pistol, ensuring he was prepared for any scenario.

Tally, her expression resolute, carefully deliberated her choices. Opting for the Remington 870 (12 gauge) Shotgun as her primary weapon, she recognized its prowess in close-quarters combat. With confidence in her marksmanship, she selected the Marlin 1895 chambered in .450 Marlin as her backup rifle.

Meanwhile, Jasper opted for a Winchester 30-30 lever action rifle as his primary firearm, known for its reliability and effectiveness in various hunting scenarios. For backup, he chose the Smith & Wesson 44 Magnum, ensuring he was prepared for any situation that might arise.

Jake relished using powerful firearms and felt thankful for having gone target shooting earlier in the week, granting him access to these types of guns.

36

TWISTED LOGIC

A s the Berne family careened down the road, their minivan hurtling through the darkened streets, they were desperate to escape the unfolding nightmare. The night had started innocently enough, with Warren, the family Patriarch, abruptly rousing their three children from their beds and ushering them into the family vehicle. His wife Cherie and his mother-in-law Margaret had followed suit, their faces etched with a mixture of confusion and terror as they scrambled to obey Warren's urgent commands.

With Margaret settled in behind Warren in the driver's seat and Cherie seated beside him, they embarked on their frantic escape, their hearts pounding with fear at the havoc erupting around them. The phone lines were dead, the intermittent flickering of the streetlights casting eerie shadows as they raced past crashed cars and the lifeless bodies strewn across the road.

Cherie's pleas for caution were lost in the roar of the engine. She begged Warren to slow down, her hands gripping the dashboard in a futile attempt to steady herself. But Warren's eyes remained fixed on the road ahead, his determination to get his family to safety overriding any concerns for their immediate well-being.

Then, in an instant, their world was torn apart. Without warning, a massive tree crashed through the windshield, the glass exploding into a shower of deadly shards. Warren and Margaret were impaled by the jagged branches, their lives extinguished in a heartbeat as the minivan careened out of control, hurtling towards its final, catastrophic collision with a nearby house.

Amidst the devastation, Cherie lay dazed and battered, her mind reeling from the horror of what had just transpired. The air was thick with the acrid scent of smoke and fear as she struggled to make sense of the nightmare unfolding around her.

Before she could fully grasp the situation, an ear-splitting roar shattered the night, and with a sickening crunch, her collarbone shattered as she was violently pulled through the shattered car window.

In that harrowing moment, Cherie found herself face to face with the creature, its massive form looming over her like a sinister apparition. Its red eyes blazed with a malevolent gleam, seeming to bore into her very soul with their intensity. With a grip as unyielding as iron, the Sasquatch seized her by the throat, effortlessly lifting her off the ground. Gasping for air, she struggled against its crushing grasp, her heart hammering with terror as she stared into those abyssal eyes.

Every fiber of her being screamed for escape as she felt the creature's monstrous strength constricting her windpipe. In her panic, she lost all semblance of control, her body convulsing with fear and helplessness. The putrid stench of its breath overwhelmed her senses, suffocating her with its foul odor.

With a force fueled by sheer malice, the Sasquatch turned and impaled her body on a jagged shard of wood from the shattered house. Agony lanced through her as she felt the splintered edge tear into her flesh, the excruciating pain eclipsing all thought save for the image of her children.

As darkness closed in around her, she clung to the memory of her loved ones, her final moments haunted by their faces as the darkness claimed her.

Having dispatched another victim, the Sasquatch shifted its attention to the minivan, its primal gaze locking onto the three children huddled inside. With a keen sense of smell, it sniffed the air, its towering figure casting a foreboding shadow over the terrified youngsters.

Deep within the recesses of its primitive mind, the Patriarch Sasquatch pondered the plight of the children. Despite the turmoil it had wrought upon their world, it felt a pang of empathy for their innocence lost. In its own twisted logic, it believed that subjecting them to a life under the reign of the Sasquatches would be a fate worse than death.

With a deep huff and a guttural grunt, it turned away, its inscrutable intentions leaving the children frozen in terror.

As the Sasquatch disappeared into the night, a solitary tear trickled down the eldest child's face, silently bearing witness to the unimaginable horrors they had witnessed and the uncertain fate that awaited them in the darkness.

37

VIGILANT

.....

As Jasper maintained his vigilant watch over the north side of the building, crouched low to avoid detection by any approaching Sasquatches, his watch read 3:30 am. With three hours until sunrise, time seemed to stretch endlessly, each passing minute weighed down by anticipation and dread.

"I never would have thought I would be standing guard, watching for Bigfoots," he muttered to himself, a wry sense of irony mingling with the gravity of their situation.

His eyes darted around, scanning every shadow and corner, until they settled on the park adjacent to the parking lot across the street. A flicker of movement caught his attention, and Jasper's gaze honed in on two crimson orbs gleaming in the darkness. They seemed to pierce through the night, fixating on him with an unsettling intensity.

Perplexed, Jasper blinked and looked again, but the red orbs remained, unwavering in their gaze. *Could it be eye shine?* he wondered silently, his heart pounding in his chest. Then, to his horror, the orbs blinked, confirming his worst fears.

"Holy crap!" Jasper's exclamation cut through the silence, drawing Jake's attention from the other side of the roof.

"What?" Jake's voice echoed back, filled with concern.

Jasper hesitated for a moment before responding, "I see large eye shine coming from a tree in the park. Do Sasquatches have red eyes?"

Jake's brow furrowed in apprehension. "Yes, they do" he queried, his voice tinged with unease. Jasper shook his head, his expression grim. "I don't know how long it has been sitting there watching us," he admitted.

A shiver ran down Jake's spine as he processed the implications. "You mean it could have been there the whole time, watching us?" he asked, his voice barely above a whisper.

Jasper shrugged, a sense of dread settling over him. "I have no idea, man," he replied, his tone tinged with fear. "But that shit is creepy as hell."

With a nod of understanding, Jake instructed, "Well, best you can do is keep an eye on it. We can't afford to let our guard down." As the weight of their situation pressed upon them, Jasper returned his focus to the looming threat in the park, his senses heightened, and his nerves on edge.

38

RUTHLESS EFFICIENCY

U nder the cloak of night, the Patriarch Sasquatch prowled the desolate streets of the town, its keen senses detecting even the faintest traces of human presence. The eerie silence was pierced only by the occasional creaking of abandoned structures and the distant echoes of screams and roars.

Inside a small trailer parked along the roadside, a family cowered in fear, their desperate whispers barely audible over the pounding of their own hearts. Seeking refuge within the cramped confines of their mobile home, they hoped to evade the horrors that lurked outside. But their hopes were dashed as the unmistakable sound of heavy footsteps reverberated outside.

With a sudden, bone-chilling thud, the Sasquatch slammed its massive fists against the metal walls of the trailer, each blow sending shock waves of terror through the trapped family. In a panic, they huddled together, their eyes wide with fear as the trailer shook violently under the creature's relentless assault.

With a deafening roar, the Sasquatch pushed against the

side of the trailer, its immense strength threatening to overturn the flimsy structure. As the trailer teetered on the brink of collapse, the Patriarch Sasquatch unleashed a final, devastating blow, sending the metal shell crashing to the ground with a cacophony of twisted metal and splintered wood, exposing the terrified family to the nightmarish reality outside.

Amidst the chaos, the Sasquatch loomed over the wreckage, its hate-filled gaze fixed on the petrified family within. With methodical precision, it began to pull each member from the debris, its massive claws tearing through flesh and bone with ruthless efficiency.

First, it seized the father, Barry, in its monstrous grip, lifting him effortlessly into the air. Barry's screams of terror were abruptly silenced as the Sasquatch delivered a crushing blow with its fist that shattered his skull like porcelain.

Next, it turned its attention to Theresa, the mother, her terrified screams piercing the night. Despite her terror, she fought back, thumping and hitting the Sasquatch, but her efforts were in vain as the creature's jagged teeth tore into her flesh, ripping her throat out with savage brutality.

Not inclined to spare the children as it had done before, the Sasquatch turned its sights onto the eldest son, Tyler. He fought desperately against the creature's grasp, but his struggles proved futile against its immense strength. With a sickening crunch, the Sasquatch snapped his spine in two, leaving him limp and lifeless in its wake.

Finally, the daughter, Emily, stood frozen with fear as the creature approached. Its eyes gleamed with rage as it moved swiftly, silencing her cries with a swift punch through her chest, leaving her body to fall amidst the remnants of the broken trailer.

As the air grew thick with the scent of death, the Patriarch Sasquatch stood amidst the carnage, its primal instincts sated for the moment as it gazed upon the devastation it had wrought.

147

39

EXTERMINATE

As the young Sasquatch observed the hairless ones from the safety of the shadows in the tree, he sensed a shift in the air, a subtle awareness that they had become aware of his presence. With calculated precision, he knew it was time to act.

In a sudden eruption of sound, he unleashed a siren-like call, a primal wail that echoed through the night. The eerie cry pierced the darkness, lasting for about 30 seconds, serving as a signal to his kin, summoning them to join him. There was no room for hesitation; the hairless ones could not be allowed to escape.

As the call reverberated through the night, the young Sasquatch's excitement grew, fueled by the thought of his tribe rallying together to confront their adversaries. The prospect of the impending battle filled him with a sense of purpose and pride.

He could hear the thunderous footsteps of his tribe members echoing through the deserted streets below. Each stride filled him with a sense of exhilaration and anticipation. Soon, he thought, this town would belong to them.

With each passing moment, the rhythmic pounding of their footsteps grew louder, signaling the imminent arrival of his kin. They moved swiftly and purposefully, a formidable force united by a common goal: to exterminate the hairless ones.

40

HAUNTING ECHOES

"What in the hell was that?" Jasper exclaimed, lowering his hands from his ears. The piercing wail of the Sasquatch reverberated through every fiber of his being, sending shivers down his spine. The intensity of the call had affected them all, and Jake suspected it was a summons for more Sasquatches to join the fray. With a sense of urgency, he rallied Jasper and Tally, their eyes mirroring the tension that gripped him.

"I fear that was a call for reinforcements," Jake asserted, his voice unwavering. "Prepare yourselves. They're on their way, and they won't hold back. Aim for their heads or legs; their chests seem to be protected by thick, matted hair. And under no circumstances let them reach the roof. We must hold our ground."

As he spoke, anticipation hung heavy in the air, each passing moment amplifying the intensity of the impending confrontation. The sound of their own breathing seemed magnified, drowned out only by the approaching footsteps of the Sasquatches. Jasper and Tally nodded in grim acknowledgment, their expressions hardened with determination. They knew the stakes were high, their survival dependent on their ability to defend the rooftop against the relentless onslaught of their monstrous adversaries.

With weapons raised and hearts pounding, they braced themselves for the inevitable clash, every nerve on edge as they awaited the imminent arrival of their fearsome foes. In the eerie stillness of the night, the tension reached its zenith, poised on the razor's edge between anticipation and dread.their

41

UNLEASH FURY

With a roar of determination, the Patriarch of the Sasquatch tribe abandoned the scene of his recent carnage, leaving behind the lifeless bodies of the family he had ruthlessly slain in a small trailer. As he charged through the moonlit streets, his massive form a blur of motion, the Patriarch's mind seethed with a singular purpose: vengeance. The calls for action echoed in his ears, driving him onward, a relentless force propelling him toward the gathering point in the park where his tribe awaited.

With each thundering footfall, his fury swelled, his resolve hardened like iron. The hairless ones would pay for their transgressions, for the blood they had spilled and the lives they had stolen. As he neared the park, the Patriarch's chest heaved with exertion, his breaths coming in ragged, primal bursts. His eyes gleamed with a fierce, unyielding fire, a sign of the burning rage that consumed him.

With a mighty roar that echoed through the night, the Patriarch signaled his arrival, his voice a rallying cry that stirred the hearts of his kin. Together, they would unleash their fury upon the hairless ones, a relentless tide of vengeance that would not be quenched until justice had been served, until every last drop of blood had been spilled in retribution for their fallen kin.

42

BEYOND THE REALM
OF NIGHTMARES

Jasper's breath caught in his throat as he gazed upon the horde of Sasquatches gathering in the street below, their massive forms towering over the abandoned cars and trucks like ancient titans of myth. Tally stood frozen beside him, her eyes wide with terror mirroring his own shock and disbelief.

The sheer size and ugliness of the creatures made Jasper shudder, a fear like no other gripping him in its icy embrace. This was beyond anything he had ever imagined, beyond the realm of nightmares into a waking hell.

"They're much bigger than I thought they would be," Jasper stammered, not believing his own eyes.

As the largest Sasquatch came to a halt, its gaze fixed upon the roof where they stood, Jasper counted at least twenty others joining in, their eyes burning with an otherworldly intensity. Even the juvenile Sasquatch that had been hiding in the tree now stood among them, its presence adding to the sense of dread that hung heavy in the air.

Jasper and Tally exchanged horrified glances, silently grappling with the magnitude of the situation unfolding before them. They were hopelessly outnumbered, facing an enemy unlike any they had ever encountered.

Beside them, Jake's voice cut through the tense silence, his words a grim reminder of their dire circumstances. "Preserve your ammunition," he urged, his tone grave. "Make every shot count. We defend our position until every last one of them is dead."

Jasper and Tally nodded in agreement, fully aware of the stakes at hand. They recognized that the longer they could hold out and the more Sasquatches they could shoot, the less attention the creatures would have for hunting down any more townspeople. With a sense of grim determination, he tightened his grip on his weapon, ready to face the impending onslaught. There was no turning back now. They would stand their ground, facing the enemy with unwavering resolve, determined to fight until their last breath.

With a thunderous roar, the Sasquatches descended upon the bar like a relentless force of nature, their unearthly cries echoing through the night. The Patriarch stood motionless, his gaze fixed upon the building where his enemies awaited.

As his fellow tribe members charged forward, some barreling into the structure in search of a way to reach the roof, the Patriarch's attention shifted to the commotion unfolding before him. A female Sasquatch leaped up towards the decking on the second floor, her claws scraping against the wooden boards in a desperate attempt to reach their prey.

Jasper, his rifle steady in his grip, reacted swiftly, taking aim and firing a shot that struck the Sasquatch square in the shoulder. The creature let out a deafening scream as it plummeted to the ground, writhing in agony.

But before Jasper could even register his success, another Sasquatch took its place, leaping up onto the decking with a feral grin. As it stood, confidence gleaming in its eyes, the wooden structure beneath it gave way with a loud crack, sending the creature crashing to the ground below in a heap of splintered wood and dust.

The scene erupted into bedlam as more Sasquatches surged forward, their primal instincts driving them to reach their prey at any cost.

Undeterred by the gunfire, the Sasquatches pressed on, some attempting to scale the walls of the building in a desperate bid to reach the trio on the roof. But with every attempt, they were met with a hail of bullets, each shot sending them tumbling back to the ground below.

Jake's .300 Winchester Magnum roared to life, its rounds tearing through the thick hair and flesh of the Sasquatches with devastating effect. Meanwhile, Jasper's .308 Winchester Magnum echoed in tandem, his shots finding their targets with lethal precision.

Tally, doing her best to fend off the relentless army of Sasquatch and trying to keep an ear on the Sasquatches in the stairwell, relied on her Remington 870 Shotgun, unleashing a barrage of slugs. Her years of hunting with her grandfather proved invaluable in this dire situation.

Rai sat in the middle of the rooftop with her hands over her ears.

Despite their best efforts, the Sasquatches continued their assault, their numbers dwindling with each volley of gunfire.

But for every beast they felled, it seemed that two more took its place.

Amongst the chaos, the Patriarch of the Sasquatch tribe stood back, watching the carnage unfold with a stoic expression. Despite the losses suffered by his kin, there was no hint of fear or hesitation in his eyes, only a steely resolve to see his mission through to the bitter end.

Jake fired tirelessly at each Sasquatch in sight, his .300 Winchester Magnum rifle overheating from the constant barrage. With six Sasquatches down, he realized they were being replaced as quickly as he could shoot them.

Calling out to Jasper and Tally, he asked how they were holding up. They barely glanced his way, focused on their own battle. They all prayed for a miracle as they fought off the onslaught. Swiftly switching to a Remington 870 (12 gauge), Jake unleashed an unyielding barrage of shots, determined to hold back the advancing horde.

Then, a thought struck Jake. He remembered the flash bangs tucked away in one of his gun bags. He had kept them to try out with Jasper and had forgotten all about them. Though he'd never needed them before, now might be the perfect time. With determination, he rushed to retrieve them, knowing he'd have to wait for the opportune moment to deploy them.not be quenched until justice had been served, until every last drop of blood had been spilled in retribution for their fallen kin.

43

FIGHT TILL THE BITTER END

As the Patriarch Sasquatch watched the battle unfold, his heart remained unburdened by the losses suffered by his tribe. To him, they were casualties of a bigger picture, sacrifices in the pursuit of a greater goal. His mind was singularly focused on revenge, on avenging the death of his mother and two children at the hands of the hairless ones.

With a commanding roar that resonated through the night, the Patriarch signaled to his remaining kin to fall back. Despite their weariness and injuries, they obeyed without question, knowing that their leader had a plan.

As they retreated to the safety of the park across the street, the Patriarch's mind raced with thoughts of vengeance. He knew that they needed a new approach, a strategy that would catch the hairless ones off guard and bring them to their knees.

The Patriarch gathered his tribe around him, his eyes burning with determination. There was no room for sadness or doubt in his mind; there was only the burning desire for revenge.

As the Sasquatches settled in to rest and regroup, the Patriarch began to formulate a new plan of attack. They would use their strength and cunning to outmaneuver their adversaries, to strike fear into the hearts of those who had dared to threaten their kin.

With a renewed sense of purpose, the Patriarch rallied his tribe, his voice booming with authority. They were ready to fight until the bitter end in pursuit of their ultimate goal: vengeance against the hairless ones who had brought death and destruction to their kind.

As the Sasquatches retreated, a sense of uneasy calm settled over Jasper, Tally, and Jake. Jasper's eyes scanned the scene, trying to make sense of the sudden change in the Sasquatches' tactics. "What are they doing?" he asked his companions, his voice tinged with apprehension.

Jake's response was grim. "I'd like to say they're giving up, but I don't think we're that lucky." His eyes remained fixed on the retreating figures, wary of any sudden movements.

Tally, her muscles aching from the relentless battle, sank down to the ground, grateful for the chance to rest. "Neither do I," she muttered, exhaustion evident in her voice. "Let's take a quick break, but keep our eyes on them."

Jake nodded in agreement, his gaze never leaving the retreating Sasquatches. "Yeah, take a breather, guys, but don't let your guard down," he warned. "They're probably coming up with another plan."

Despite the momentary respite, tension hung heavy in the air, each of them acutely aware that the Sasquatches were far from defeated. They knew that they couldn't afford to let their guard down, not even for a moment, if they hoped to survive whatever the Sasquatches had in store for them next.

As Jake took a swig of water, replenishing his parched throat, Tally checked on Rai, ensuring the young girl was holding up amid the chaos. As he set his water bottle down, his gaze swept across the surroundings, ever vigilant for any sign of danger. Suddenly, his attention was drawn to a lone figure darting down the lane way adjacent to the bar.

His heart pounded with uncertainty. Was this newcomer friend or foe? Had they come to offer aid, or were they drawn by the sound of gunfire, seeking to plunder their weapons?

Jake motioned for Jasper to join him, his eyes fixed on the approaching figure. As the figure emerged into the dim light of a street lamp, Jasper said excitedly, "That's my Dad! Oh my god!"

Jake felt a surge of relief wash over him as Jasper's father, Francis, waved up to them. However, a pressing question lingered: how could they ensure his safety by bringing him up to the roof?

Reacting swiftly, Jake turned to Jasper. "Jasper, we need that makeshift rope we used for the piano. Can you grab it from the storage room?" he asked urgently. Jasper nodded in understanding and hurried off to retrieve the rope. Moments later, he returned with the rope in hand, tossing it down to his father below.

While Tally kept watch on the Sasquatch, with a sense of urgency, Jasper's father tied the rope securely around his waist, ready to be hoisted up. Jake and Jasper hurriedly pulled on the rope, their hearts racing with apprehension. They couldn't afford to be discovered by the Sasquatches.

With each tug, they brought Jasper's father closer to safety. As he was pulled onto the roof, the men shared a moment of relief, catching their breath after the tense ordeal. Jasper rushed forward, embracing his father tightly, grateful for his arrival in their hour of need.

As Francis recounted the harrowing events he witnessed, Jasper listened intently, a mix of relief and sorrow washing over him. "Dad, you did the right thing, and I'm so glad you're alive," Jasper said, his voice filled with gratitude.

Tears welled in Francis's eyes as he continued, his voice trembling with emotion. "It had been quiet for a while so I gathered up the courage to come and find you. I assumed you would be at the bar, well at least I hoped you would be."

"We're glad to have you here, Mr. Bosher," Jake interjected, offering his support. "Oh Jake, you know you can call me Francis by now," Francis replied with a faint smile.

"Alright, Francis," Jake nodded, acknowledging the familiarity. "We've held out here for a few hours. The Sasquatches have been relentless, but they retreated to the park over there. We assume they're regrouping and planning their next move. We're hoping to hold out until sunrise, hoping help will arrive then."

"You're welcome to grab a gun from the bag over there," Jake offered, gesturing towards the nearby equipment.

Francis nodded, a determined glint in his eyes. "I'll stick with my trusty 30-06," he declared confidently. "With its 180 grain bullets, it should do the trick."

"Alright, I'm going back to keep an eye on the south side," Jake announced. "Jasper's manning the east. If you want to take the west, that would be very helpful."

Francis nodded, grateful for the opportunity to contribute to their defense.

44

VICTORY OR DEATH

As the first light of dawn began to creep over the horizon, casting a faint glow across the landscape, the Patriarch Sasquatch stood tall amidst his remaining tribe members. The urgency of their situation weighed heavily upon him, the dwindling darkness serving as a reminder that time was running out. With each passing moment, the threat of daylight grew stronger, urging them to act swiftly and decisively.

With a commanding presence, the Patriarch gathered his fellow Sasquatches, their eyes gleaming with fierce determination.

In their ancient language, a symphony of grunts, clicks, and gestures, the Patriarch outlined their new strategy. Every member of the tribe listened intently, their anticipation growing with each word. They hung on his every gesture, their muscles tense with anticipation as they awaited their orders.

The Patriarch's words carried the weight of their collective anger and resentment, each syllable dripping with defiance against their oppressors. He reminded them of the losses they had suffered, the lives taken by the hairless ones. The Sasquatches' fury swelled, and they were ready for revenge.

With a thunderous roar that reverberated through the streets, the Sasquatches scattered, their movements swift and purposeful. The air buzzed with anticipation as they prepared to unleash their fury upon the hairless ones once more, their primal instincts guiding them toward victory or death.

45

FINAL STAND

....

As the Sasquatches grew more excited, Jasper shouted to Jake to join his side. They could hear the rumble of the Sasquatches' chatter, a tumult of primal fury filling the air.

"The leader is getting them riled up," Jake said, his voice tense with urgency. "They're definitely planning something."

Suddenly, the leader threw back its head, unleashing an ear-splitting scream that reverberated through the air. Then, with a surge of energy, some of the Sasquatches charged forward while others dispersed, their intentions unclear.

Tally, her eyes wide with alarm, questioned, "What are they doing?" Her query was answered moments later as a rock hurtled past, narrowly missing her by mere inches. "That's your answer," Francis warned, his voice grim. "Get down low, people. They're throwing rocks."

With a sense of urgency, Jake took up his position and began firing at the oncoming Sasquatches. His heart pounded in his chest as he watched in disbelief as one of them quickly scaled the wall of the structure, aided by its comrades. They were working together, their intelligence far surpassing what they had expected.

Frozen in shock for a moment, Jake snapped back to reality and resumed firing his gun. His shots found their marks with deadly accuracy, taking down the Sasquatches one by one. His heart raced as he watched in grim satisfaction as the top Sasquatch met its demise, its eyes and nose obliterated by Jake's bullets.

Meanwhile, Francis remained vigilant, dodging rocks and keeping a watchful eye on the attic door. He knew that if the Sasquatches breached that door, it would spell the end for all of them.

Jasper, his nerves frayed with adrenaline, continued to fire at the advancing Sasquatches. His shot hit the leader square in the ribs, eliciting a roar of pain. The Sasquatch turned its gaze towards Jasper, its eyes burning with fury as it prepared to retaliate.

The Patriarch Sasquatch charged with terrifying speed towards the ruins of the decking strewn across the road outside the bar. Grabbing a wooden paling, it hurled it like a spear at Jasper, who narrowly dodged it, the projectile grazing his shoulder. The shock of the near miss elicited a scream from him, more from sheer terror than pain.

In a frenzy, th remaining Sasquatches joined in, launching wood projectiles with lightning speed at the hairless ones.

As Francis reloaded, he kept a wary eye on the incoming projectiles, dodging with a grace borne of adrenaline. But in the heat of battle, not every move goes as planned. A misstep—a foot caught on an unseen piece of debris—sent Francis tumbling forward, his world suddenly skewing as he found himself falling over the edge of the rooftop they had fought so hard to defend.

The fall seemed to stretch, time dilating around him as he saw the ground rush up to meet him. As Francis hit the ground with a bone-jarring thud, the world around him blurred into a feeling of pain and disorientation. He could feel the jagged edge of reality as his bones protested with fractures too numerous to count. Through the ringing in his ears, he could faintly discern Jasper's voice, filled with panic and dread, screaming his name. It was a sound that seemed to come from far away. Francis tried to move, to respond to that familiar voice, but his body was a prison of pain, unyielding and unresponsive.

Then, looming above him, the Patriarch approached, its massive form casting a shadow that enveloped Francis in darkness. For a fleeting moment, they made eye contact, and Francis knew his time was near, the predator closing in on its prey. With a force that seemed to shake the very earth, the Sasquatch brought its foot down upon Francis's face. The world went silent for him then, the screaming, the gunfire, and the chaos fading into nothingness.

Tally was crying and holding back Jasper, who was screaming, his voice raw with despair, as he watched his father be mercilessly killed by the Sasquatch. A feeling of helplessness engulfed Jasper. He was devastated, witnessing the unthinkable loss of his father in such a horrifying way, a moment that would forever leave a scar upon his heart.

Reeling from the shock of Francis's loss, Jake recognized the critical opportunity before them. He quickly briefed Tally and Jasper about the flash bangs, explaining that this was their moment to potentially end the threat of the Sasquatches once and for all.

With the creatures distracted by their ongoing assault, he saw a chance for a decisive counterattack. Jake grabbed the flash bangs and urgently instructed the others to protect their eyes and ears. Despite their initial confusion, Tally and Jasper trusted Jake's command and prepared themselves and Rai as he launched two flash bangs directly into the Sasquatch group.

The resulting blinding light and deafening roar threw the remaining Sasquatches into disarray, offering the perfect moment for a counterstrike.

"Shoot them now!" Jake yelled over the ringing in his ears. Without a second's hesitation, Tally and Jasper responded, unleashing a barrage of bullets into the disoriented creatures.

Bullets tore through flesh and limb, leaving devastation in their wake. The Sasquatches stood no chance against the onslaught, their bodies ripped apart by the relentless barrage.

Amidst the mayhem, Jake spotted the Patriarch attempting to flee. Determined not to let it escape, he took aim and fired, shattering its right knee with a well-aimed shot. The creature roared in agony, clutching at its mangled limb. Jake didn't relent, firing again to take out the other knee, blood spraying in all directions.

As the Patriarch Sasquatch crumpled to the ground, its powerful legs rendered useless, it emitted a guttural growl that reverberated through the air. With a malevolent glare fixed upon Jake, a chill raced down his spine, freezing him in place with a innate fear. Without hesitation, Jake steadied his aim just below the chin of the downed creature. As he fired, Jake shouted a defiant "Fuck you" to the Sasquatch. The bullet sliced through flesh and bone, devastating the Sasquatch's throat in a gruesome spray of gore, ensuring there would be no recovery.

But Jake knew he couldn't take any chances. With a final,

fatal shot to the nose, he ended the Patriarch's life, the bullet piercing through soft tissue and finding its mark in the creature's brain, exploding its head into a gruesome mess over the pavement.

46

SCARS OF THE NIGHT

As the last echoes of gunfire faded into the dawn, an eerie calm settled over the scene. The once chaotic streets now lay silent, save for the occasional creak of damaged buildings. Jasper and Tally, their breath still labored from the intense battle, exchanged a solemn nod.

Meanwhile, Jake, overcome by exhaustion, sank to the ground, his body trembling with fatigue. The weight of the night's events bore down upon him, leaving him physically and mentally drained. He closed his eyes briefly, attempting to steady his ragged breathing and calm his racing thoughts.

As Jasper's sharp and vigilant eyes scanned the surrounding area for any lingering threats, grief weighed heavy on his heart. The memory of his father's death left a deep wound that would linger for the rest of his life. Nonetheless, he pressed forward, determined to protect those he still held dear.

Satisfied that the immediate danger had passed, he approached Tally, his footsteps echoing with weariness but also with a sense of relief.

Without a word, Tally embraced him in a long, heartfelt hug. Rai, clinging to Tally's leg, looked up at Jasper with wide eyes, her expression a blend of gratitude for being saved and sorrow for the loss they had suffered.

As the sun crept ever closer to the horizon, casting its warm rays upon the battered streets, Jake, Jasper, Tally, and Rai sat in silence, their weary eyes fixed on the scene unfolding before them. It was a remarkable sight: survivors emerging cautiously from their hiding places, venturing into the open with tentative steps. Some limped from injuries sustained during the carnage, while others carried the weight of fear etched into their faces like visible scars.

With each passing moment, more survivors joined them in the streets. Though the scars of the night would forever linger, they stood united in their survival, ready to rebuild and reclaim their town from the beats that had threatened to consume it.

47

AFTERMATH

....

T he arrival of government officials, accompanied by law enforcement, just after dawn signaled a swift mobilization to rid the streets of any evidence of the Sasquatches' presence. Their urgency was evident as bulldozers roared to life and workers rushed to carry out their directives. The town's residents watched with a mixture of apprehension and resignation, recognizing the stark reminder of power dynamics at play.

As heavy machinery cleared away debris and workers toiled to repair shattered buildings, the once vibrant streets bore the marks of destruction. The usual hum of activity was replaced by the clamor of cleanup crews and the steady rhythm of government agencies. Each hammer blow and revving engine served as a poignant reminder of the harrowing events that had unfolded, etching themselves into the collective memory of the town.

Amongst the aftermath, whispers of disbelief permeated through social media channels, fueling speculation and doubt. Rumors of a cover-up tale concocted by the authorities spread like wildfire, weaving a dubious narrative of rabid bears terrorizing the town's residents. Skepticism mingled with fear as the townsfolk grappled with the unsettling truth behind the facade of official explanations.

A quiet consensus had emerged quickly amongst the townsfolk. It was deemed best to keep the truth buried, a decision born out of necessity rather than deceit. The specter of further conflict and the prospect of attracting unwanted attention loomed large in their minds, prompting a collective agreement to maintain a facade of normalcy, however fragile it may be. The fear of sensationalism and the possibility of attracting hundreds of individuals in search of Sasquatches weighed heavily on their hearts, driving them to guard their secrets closely and shield their already fragile town from prying eyes.

In the midst of this delicate balance, Rai found comfort and familiarity in the embrace of her aunt, a calming presence amidst the turmoil. Together, they navigated the turbulent aftermath, finding strength in their bond amidst the overwhelming grief that threatened to consume them.

Tally, her eyes reflecting a mixture of determination and sorrow, made a sincere promise to Rai. Despite the challenges that lay ahead, she vowed to check in on her regularly, ensuring her well-being.

As Jasper grappled with the overwhelming grief of losing his father, Jake stood by his side, offering unwavering support during the difficult process of arranging the funeral. Together, they navigated the intricate details, from selecting the casket to coordinating with the funeral home.

However, through their sorrow, a harsh reality loomed: the local coroner, overwhelmed by the sheer number of bodies to process, had to call in additional help from neighboring jurisdictions. The task ahead was daunting and would undoubtedly be long and arduous, as each life lost during the reckoning needed to be properly documented and accounted for.

Consequently, Jasper would have to wait longer than expected to bid his final farewell to his father, as the funeral arrangements were delayed due to the coroner's overwhelming workload.

48

FAMILY PRIORITIES

A s the sun dipped below the horizon, casting long shadows across the quiet streets of Sutter Creek, Jake and Jasper found themselves seated at a diner in town. Having been spared in the destruction of the town, the atmosphere was subdued, with only the sporadic clinking of cutlery and soft murmurs of conversation breaking the silence.

"Jasper," Jake began, his voice steady but tinged with empathy, "I've made some arrangements."

Jasper looked up, meeting Jake's gaze with a mixture of curiosity and apprehension. "What kind of arrangements?" he asked, his voice barely above a whisper.

Jake took a moment to collect his thoughts before continuing. "I've called my work," he explained, "and I've told them that I'll need to take care of business here for another week or two. I want to stay in Sutter Creek to help with cleaning up the bar and to support you through your grief."

Jasper's eyes widened in surprise, gratitude washing over him like a wave. "Jake, you don't have to do that," he protested, his voice choked with emotion. "You have your own life to get back to."

Jake reached out, placing a reassuring hand on Jasper's shoulder. "I know I don't have to," he said softly, "but I want to. You're family, Jasper. And family takes care of each other."

A faint smile tugged at the corners of Jake's lips as he continued, a hint of levity creeping into his tone. "Plus," he added with a playful glint in his eye, "being the boss does have its perks. I get to decide if I get time off or not, and I've decided that right now, my priority is right here in Sutter Creek."

Tears welled up in Jasper's eyes as he struggled to find the words to express his gratitude. "Thank you, Jake," he managed to choke out, his voice thick with emotion. "You are a great friend."

Jake squeezed Jasper's shoulder gently, a silent gesture of solidarity. "I'm here for you, buddy," he said firmly. "All the way."

49

THE FALLEN

s the days turned into weeks, the Sasquatches who had remained behind awaited the return of their kin with growing apprehension. They had watched them depart with a mixture of pride and worry, knowing that they ventured into danger to protect their home and family. But as the days passed without any sign of their return, a heavy silence settled over the group, broken only by the mournful howls of the wind.

The Matriarch, once a pillar of strength and resilience, now found herself consumed by grief. The loss of her children had left a void in her heart that could never be filled, and now, with the added anguish of losing her partner, she felt adrift in a sea of sorrow. Each day, she went about her chores with a heavy heart, her eyes scanning the paths in the forest for any sign of her beloved.

The days stretched into weeks, and hope began to wane. The harsh reality of their situation weighed heavily on the group, their once-unbreakable bond now frayed by the pain of loss. The Matriarch, in particular, felt the weight of her grief like a physical burden, each step a struggle against the crushing weight of despair.

Yet, amidst the darkness, a glimmer of resilience remained. Despite her overwhelming sorrow, the Matriarch continued to perform her duties with unwavering determination. She gathered food for the group, tended to their shelter, and watched over them with a silent vigilance. It was a silent tribute to the love she had lost.

The Matriarch knew deep down that her partner would not return, that he had fallen in battle like so many others. And yet, she could not bring herself to accept it. Each day, she looked up at the sky, her heart heavy with longing, hoping against hope that he would come back to her.

The passage of time only served to deepen the sense of loss that pervaded the Sasquatch tribe. It had become increasingly apparent that their loved ones would never come back.

With a heavy heart and tears in her eyes, the Matriarch was forced to confront the harsh reality of her situation. Her beloved partner was gone, lost to the merciless tide of war. The grief that weighed upon her was almost unbearable, a crushing burden that threatened to consume her whole.

Though their losses were great, the tribe endured, their resilience a testament to the strength of their spirit. But it would take time—perhaps even decades—for them to recover from the devastation wrought by the conflict.

With heads held high, the Sasquatch tribe embarked on the long road to recovery. Though the scars of war would never fully heal, they knew that their loved ones would always be with them, watching over them from the great beyond.

EPILOGUE

PATH TO NORMALCY

As Jake's car hummed along the familiar stretch of highway, his thoughts drifted back to the events that had unfolded in Sutter Creek. The road seemed to stretch endlessly before him, mirroring the journey he had embarked upon in the wake of the town's ordeal.

The weight of the past two weeks settled heavily on his shoulders, a burden he carried with a mix of sorrow and resolve. The memories of the battle, the grief, and the strengthening of bonds amidst the turmoil lingered in his mind, refusing to be easily shaken off.

After moving out of the watchtower into Jasper's house, it had provided a semblance of normalcy amidst the whirlwind of the past few weeks. Together, and with Tally's help, they had worked tirelessly to restore the bar, transforming it from a shattered shell into a beacon of resilience and hope for the town's future. The sound of hammering and the scent of fresh paint had filled the air, they were determined to rebuild what had been lost.

The piano, which undoubtedly helped shield them from the Sasquatches by blocking the stairwell to the rooftop, now rested in the band area of the bar, serving as a reminder of their resilience and unity.

The funeral for Jasper's father, Francis, had been a sad yet cathartic occasion. Standing beside his friend as they bid farewell to a loved one had stirred up a myriad of emotions within Jake. The sight of the townsfolk gathered together, united in their grief, had been both heartbreaking and comforting, a reminder of the strength found in community.

During his last days in Sutter Creek, Jake had also received news of his own father's passing. The sudden realization had stirred up a whirlwind of conflicting emotions within him. While he hadn't had the best relationship with his father, the news still hit him harder than he had expected.

Now, as he made his way back to San Francisco, the road ahead seemed to stretch out before him like a path to normalcy. It was time to return to work, to resume his routine, and to process all that had transpired in Sutter Creek.

But amidst the familiar sights and sounds of the city, the memories of the harrowing ordeal would linger, serving as a constant reminder of the fragility of life and the strength found in community and friendship.

AUTHOR BIO

....

Luka T. Jacobs is an author with a passion for cryptids, particularly Sasquatch and Dogman. Originally hailing from Sydney, Australia, Luka now calls the picturesque Illawarra region of New South Wales home, where she resides with her partner and their cheeky little dog, Finnigan.

With a deep love for animals and a keen sense of adventure, Luka's fascination with the mysteries of the natural world fuels her storytelling. Drawing from her background in Graphic Design and Art, she brings a unique visual flair to her writing.

"Watchtower Reckoning" marks Luka's second novel, showcasing her talent for crafting gripping tales that blend elements of horror, suspense, and the supernatural. As an avid traveler and explorer of the unknown, Luka continues to seek inspiration from the wild and untamed corners of the world, eager to share her imaginative worlds with readers everywhere.

Facebook: https://www.facebook.com/lukatjacobs

Amazon: https://www.amazon.com/stores/Luka-T-Jacobs/author/B0CYW9MCG7

EMBRACE THE MYSTERY
WEAR THE LEGEND

Whether you're a fellow cryptid enthusiast, a lover of mysteries, or someone who appreciates unique, conversation-starting apparel, you'll love **The Cryptid Store**.

Our collection of **cryptid-themed merchandise** is designed to ignite imagination, raise awareness, and celebrate the mysterious creatures of this world.

Take a sneak peak at Luka T. Jacob's first novel ***"Night Of The Dogman: A Fight For Survival"*** only **available at Amazon.com** for Kindle, paperback and hard cover.

SNEAK PEAK –
NIGHT OF THE DOGMAN:
THE SCENT

The night was draped in darkness, the moon obscured by thick, swirling clouds that seemed to dance with an otherworldly energy. The Dogman moved silently through the dense undergrowth, its senses keenly attuned to the faintest sound or scent that drifted on the air.

It had parted ways with its sibling under the cover of night, a silent understanding passing between them as they each embarked on their solitary hunts. For the Dogman, the urge to roam alone was primal, an insatiable hunger that gnawed at its very core.

As it prowled through the forest, the Dogman felt a surge of exhilaration coursing through its veins. There was a thrill in the hunt, a dark pleasure that pulsed with each beat of its heart. It relished the anticipation of the chase, the moment when prey and predator collided in a deadly dance.

But there was something more to the Dogman's hunger

than mere sustenance. It craved the fear and desperation of its victims, the sweet taste of terror that lingered in the air like a tantalizing perfume. It reveled in the power it held over its prey, the way their eyes widened with horror as they realized their fate was sealed.

As the night wore on, the Dogman's hunger only grew stronger, driving it further outside its home range in search of its next meal. It moved with a fluid grace, its movements silent and predatory as it stalked through the shadows.

But even as the first faint light of dawn began to creep over the horizon, the Dogman showed no signs of slowing. It was a creature of the night, and the night was its domain. With a hunger that could never be sated, it continued to roam, driven by an insatiable thirst for blood and terror.

As the sun began to rise, casting long, ominous shadows across the forest floor, the Dogman found itself on the outskirts of a town. It paused for a moment, its senses tingling with anticipation as it contemplated what the town might offer to satisfy its dark desires.

It knew that preying on the non-hairy ones within the town limits would draw unwanted attention upon itself. The last thing it needed was the scrutiny of the non-hairy ones with their metal sticks that roar and their endless pursuit of vengeance, recalling the sensation of being shot by one of those roaring sticks a few moons ago.

With a growl of frustration, the Dogman made a calculated decision to steer clear of the town for now. It would be more prudent to remain on the outskirts, where it could hunt without fear of discovery.

As it prowled along the fringes of civilization, the Dogman's keen eyes scanned the landscape for signs of life. It was searching for a challenge, something worthy of its cunning and strength.

Suddenly, a scent caught its attention—a scent unlike any it had encountered before. It was the scent of fear, but mingled with something else, something more elusive and intriguing.

Curiosity piqued, the Dogman followed the scent, its senses ablaze with anticipation. It moved with a purpose now, driven by a primal urge to uncover the source of this mysterious scent.

As it ran across the lonely fields, the Dogman's excitement grew. It could sense that it was drawing closer to its quarry, that soon it would come face to face with the challenge it had been seeking.

With each step, the Dogman's anticipation mounted. It knew that whatever lay ahead would test its strength and intelligence to the limit. But it was ready. It was prepared to face whatever challenges its prey had in store.

SNEAK PEAK –
NIGHT OF THE DOGMAN:
A STRANGE SIGHTING

Aweek went by without incident. Adam sat on his porch, the warmth of his coffee mug cradled in his hands as he watched the sunrise paint the sky in shades of pink and gold. Fletcher lay at his feet, contentedly gnawing on a stick, unaware of the events about to unfold.

The wildlife of the Southern Missouri countryside stirred around him—the rustle of leaves as deer passed through the trees, the distant call of a bobcat, the quick darting movement of a raccoon. It was a scene familiar to Adam, a part of the rhythm of his daily life.

As Adam sat on his porch, his mind wandered back to his past life, reminiscing about the last time he felt truly content. It was a vivid memory of a day spent at the water park with Amber and Layla, just a week before their untimely deaths. The joyous laughter and playful splashing of his wife and daughter had warmed his heart in a way nothing else could. He cherished those memories of his family, holding them close like precious treasures in the depths of his soul.

Adam was lost in thought, his gaze unfocused, when something caught his eye—a dark figure swiftly moving across the rolling hills in the distance. Initially dismissing it as a trick of the light or a mere figment of his imagination, Adam's unease grew as he continued to watch. A chill ran down his spine.

Instinctively, Adam reached for the binoculars he kept nearby, raising them to his eyes and zooming in on the mysterious creature. It resembled a large coyote or coydog, its sleek black fur glistening in the morning sunlight. But there was something unsettling about it, something that filled Adam with a sense of dread.

As the creature ran, Adam could see the muscles rippling beneath its fur, the dog-like muzzle and large ears that marked it as a predator of the wilderness. But it was what happened next that caused his heart to skip a beat.

The creature halted abruptly, its gaze locking with Adam's across the distance. Then, to Adam's horror, it effortlessly rose onto two legs, displaying an eerie sense of comfort in its posture. Time seemed suspended as Adam stared into the creature's dark, penetrating eyes, witnessing it sniffing the air, igniting a primal fear within him. Adam couldn't believe what his eyes were seeing.

"What the heck is that?," he whispered to himself, the words barely audible over the pounding of his heart.

Its head resembled a mix of a wolf and a German shepherd. Its coat appeared pristine, thick, and dark, likely dark brown or black depending on the light. Even from afar, Adam noticed its fur gently swaying in the breeze, its muscular and powerful body adorned with broad shoulders and sturdy legs. Its eyes, hazel or yellow, held a predatory gleam. Its elongated, muscular arms culminated in razor-sharp claws, exuding a menacing aura. Despite the distance and lack of size comparison, Adam could discern the creature's immense size.

And then, as suddenly as it had appeared, the creature dropped back to all fours and continued on its way, disappearing into the trees beyond. Adam sat frozen on the porch, his mind reeling with disbelief at what he had just witnessed.

Fletcher stirred at his feet, sensing his master's unease, but Adam could only stare off into the distance, his thoughts consumed by the encounter. A feeling of foreboding enveloped him like a heavy shroud, darkening the once tranquil surroundings.

Adam rose from his seat and made his way inside, the image of the mysterious creature burned into his mind. As he closed the door behind him, questions lingered in his thoughts: "*Why did that animal make me feel so fearful, like I hadn't felt before? It looked like a werewolf, but those aren't real!*" Despite his rationalizations, a lingering unease settled in his gut. He knew that something had changed, that the tranquility of his solitary existence had been shattered by the presence of something dark and unknown lurking in the shadows of the Southern Missouri wilderness.

"*Night Of The Dogman: A Fight For Survival*" only **available at Amazon.com** for Kindle, paperback and hard cover.

Dear Reader,

Thank you for selecting my book from the myriad of options available. Your choice to explore my work is deeply appreciated, and your support means the world to me.

If you've found the book enjoyable, I would be grateful for your help in sharing it with others and leaving a review.

As a self-published author, reviews and word-of-mouth recommendations are vital for reaching new readers and spreading the book's message to a broader audience.